PENGUIN POPULAR CLASSICS

JULIUS CAESAR
BY WILLIAM SHAKESPEARE

PENGUIN POPULAR CLASSICS

JULIUS CAESAR

WILLIAM SHAKESPEARE

PENGUIN BOOKS
A PENGUIN/GODFREY CAVE EDITION

PENGUIN BOOKS

Published by the Penguin Group
Penguin Books Ltd, 27 Wrights Lane, London W8 5TZ, England
Penguin Books USA Inc., 375 Hudson Street, New York, New York 10014, USA
Penguin Books Australia Ltd, Ringwood, Victoria, Australia
Penguin Books Canada Ltd, 10 Alcorn Avenue, Toronto, Ontario, Canada M4V 3B2
Penguin Books (NZ) Ltd, 182–190 Wairau Road, Auckland 10, New Zealand

Penguin Books Ltd, Registered Offices: Harmondsworth, Middlesex, England

Published in Penguin Popular Classics 1994
1 3 5 7 9 10 8 6 4 2

Printed in England by Clays Ltd, St Ives plc

CONTENTS

THE WORKS OF SHAKESPEARE

APPROXIMATE DATE	PLAYS	FIRST PRINTED
Before 1594	HENRY VI *three parts*	*Folio* 1623
	RICHARD III	1597
	TITUS ANDRONICUS	1594
	LOVE'S LABOUR'S LOST	1598
	THE TWO GENTLEMEN OF VERONA	*Folio*
	THE COMEDY OF ERRORS	*Folio*
	THE TAMING OF THE SHREW	*Folio*
1594–1597	ROMEO AND JULIET (*pirated* 1597)	1599
	A MIDSUMMER NIGHT'S DREAM	1600
	RICHARD II	1597
	KING JOHN	*Folio*
	THE MERCHANT OF VENICE	1600
1597–1600	HENRY IV *part i*	1598
	HENRY IV *part ii*	1600
	HENRY V (*pirated* 1600)	*Folio*
	MUCH ADO ABOUT NOTHING	1600
	MERRY WIVES OF WINDSOR (*pirated* 1602)	*Folio*
	AS YOU LIKE IT	*Folio*
	JULIUS CAESAR	*Folio*
	TROYLUS AND CRESSIDA	1609
1601–1608	HAMLET (*pirated* 1603)	1604
	TWELFTH NIGHT	*Folio*
	MEASURE FOR MEASURE	*Folio*
	ALL'S WELL THAT ENDS WELL	*Folio*
	OTHELLO	1622
	LEAR	1608
	MACBETH	*Folio*
	TIMON OF ATHENS	*Folio*
	ANTONY AND CLEOPATRA	*Folio*
	CORIOLANUS	*Folio*
After 1608	PERICLES (*omitted from the Folio*)	1609
	CYMBELINE	*Folio*
	THE WINTER'S TALE	*Folio*
	THE TEMPEST	*Folio*
	HENRY VIII	*Folio*

POEMS

DATES UNKNOWN		
	VENUS AND ADONIS	1593
	THE RAPE OF LUCRECE	1594
	SONNETS	
	A LOVER'S COMPLAINT }	1609
	THE PHOENIX AND THE TURTLE	1601

WILLIAM SHAKESPEARE

William Shakespeare was born at Stratford upon Avon in April, 1564. He was the third child, and eldest son, of John Shakespeare and Mary Arden. His father was one of the most prosperous men of Stratford, who held in turn the chief offices in the town. His mother was of gentle birth, the daughter of Robert Arden of Wilmcote. In December, 1582, Shakespeare married Ann Hathaway, daughter of a farmer of Shottery, near Stratford; their first child Susanna was baptized on May 6, 1583, and twins, Hamnet and Judith, on February 22, 1585. Little is known of Shakespeare's early life; but it is unlikely that a writer who dramatized such an incomparable range and variety of human kinds and experiences should have spent his early manhood entirely in placid pursuits in a country town. There is one tradition, not universally accepted, that he fled from Stratford because he was in trouble for deer stealing, and had fallen foul of Sir Thomas Lucy, the local magnate; another that he was for some time a schoolmaster.

From 1592 onwards the records are much fuller. In March, 1592, the Lord Strange's players produced a new play at the Rose Theatre called *Harry the Sixth*, which was very successful, and was probably the *First Part of Henry VI*. In the autumn of 1592 Robert Greene, the best known of the professional writers, as he was dying wrote a letter to three fellow writers in which he warned them against the ingratitude of players in general, and in particular against an 'upstart crow' who 'supposes he is as much able to bombast out a blank verse as the best of you: and being an absolute Johannes Factotum is in his own conceit the only

Shake-scene in a country.' This is the first reference to Shakespeare, and the whole passage suggests that Shakespeare had become suddenly famous as a playwright. At this time Shakespeare was brought into touch with Edward Alleyne the great tragedian, and Christopher Marlowe, whose thundering parts of Tamburlaine, the Jew of Malta, and Dr Faustus Alleyne was acting, as well as Hieronimo, the hero of Kyd's *Spanish Tragedy*, the most famous of all Elizabethan plays.

In April, 1593, Shakespeare published his poem *Venus and Adonis*, which was dedicated to the young Earl of Southampton: it was a great and lasting success, and was reprinted nine times in the next few years. In May, 1594, his second poem, *The Rape of Lucrece*, was also dedicated to Southampton.

There was little playing in 1593, for the theatres were shut during a severe outbreak of the plague; but in the autumn of 1594, when the plague ceased, the playing companies were reorganized, and Shakespeare became a sharer in the Lord Chamberlain's company who went to play in the Theatre in Shoreditch. During these months Marlowe and Kyd had died. Shakespeare was thus for a time without a rival. He had already written the three parts of *Henry VI, Richard III, Titus Andronicus, The Two Gentlemen of Verona, Love's Labour's Lost, The Comedy of Errors,* and *The Taming of the Shrew*. Soon afterwards he wrote the first of his greater plays – *Romeo and Juliet* – and he followed this success in the next three years with *A Midsummer Night's Dream, Richard II,* and *The Merchant of Venice*. The two parts of *Henry IV*, introducing Falstaff, the most popular of all his comic characters, were written in 1597-8.

The company left the Theatre in 1597 owing to disputes over a renewal of the ground lease, and went to play at the

Curtain in the same neighbourhood. The disputes contin-
ued throughout 1598, and at Christmas the players settled
the matter by demolishing the old Theatre and re-erecting
a new playhouse on the South bank of the Thames, near
Southwark Cathedral. This playhouse was named the
Globe. The expenses of the new building were shared by
the chief members of the Company, including Shakespeare,
who was now a man of some means. In 1596 he had bought
New Place, a large house in the centre of Stratford, for £60,
and through his father purchased a coat-of-arms from the
Heralds, which was the official recognition that he and his
family were gentlefolk.

By the summer of 1598 Shakespeare was recognized as
the greatest of English dramatists. Booksellers were printing his more popular plays, at times even in pirated or stolen
versions, and he received a remarkable tribute from a young
writer named Francis Meres, in his book *Palladis Tamia*. In
a long catalogue of English authors Meres gave Shakespeare
more prominence than any other writer, and mentioned by
name twelve of his plays.

Shortly before the Globe was opened, Shakespeare had
completed the cycle of plays dealing with the whole story
of the Wars of the Roses with *Henry V*. It was followed by
As You Like it, and *Julius Caesar*, the first of the maturer
tragedies. In the next three years he wrote *Troilus and
Cressida*, *The Merry Wives of Windsor*, *Hamlet*, and *Twelfth
Night*.

On March 24, 1603, Queen Elizabeth died. The company
had often performed before her, but they found her suc-
cessor a far more enthusiastic patron. One of the first acts
of King James was to take over the company and to pro-
mote them to be his own servants, so that henceforward
they were known as the King's Men. They acted now very

frequently at Court, and prospered accordingly. In the early years of the reign Shakespeare wrote the more sombre comedies, *All's Well that Ends Well*, and *Measure for Measure*, which were followed by *Othello, Macbeth*, and *King Lear*. Then he returned to Roman themes with *Antony and Cleopatra* and *Coriolanus*.

Since 1601 Shakespeare had been writing less, and there were now a number of rival dramatists who were introducing new styles of drama, particularly Ben Jonson (whose first successful comedy, *Every Man in his Humour*, was acted by Shakespeare's company in 1598), Chapman, Dekker, Marston, and Beaumont and Fletcher who began to write in 1607. In 1608 the King's Men acquired a second playhouse, an indoor private theatre in the fashionable quarter of the Blackfriars. At private theatres, plays were performed indoors; the prices charged were higher than in the public playhouses, and the audience consequently was more select. Shakespeare seems to have retired from the stage about this time: his name does not occur in the various lists of players after 1607. Henceforward he lived for the most part at Stratford, where he was regarded as one of the most important citizens. He still wrote a few plays, and he tried his hand at the new form of tragi-comedy – a play with tragic incidents but a happy ending – which Beaumont and Fletcher had popularized. He wrote four of these – *Pericles, Cymbeline, The Winter's Tale*, and *The Tempest*, which was acted at Court in 1611. For the last four years of his life he lived in retirement. His son Hamnet had died in 1596: his two daughters were now married. Shakespeare died at Stratford upon Avon on April 23, 1616, and was buried in the chancel of the church, before the high altar. Shortly afterwards a memorial which still exists, with a portrait bust, was set up on the North wall. His wife survived him.

When Shakespeare died fourteen of his plays had been separately published in Quarto booklets. In 1623 his surviving fellow actors, John Heming and Henry Condell, with the co-operation of a number of printers, published a collected edition of thirty-six plays in one Folio volume, with an engraved portrait, memorial verses by Ben Jonson and others, and an Epistle to the Reader in which Heming and Condell make the interesting note that Shakespeare's 'hand and mind went together, and what he thought, he uttered with that easiness that we have scarce received from him a blot in his papers.'

The plays as printed in the Quartos or the Folio differ considerably from the usual modern text. They are often not divided into scenes, and sometimes not even into acts. Nor are there place-headings at the beginning of each scene, because in the Elizabethan theatre there was no scenery. They are carelessly printed and the spelling is erratic.

THE ELIZABETHAN THEATRE

Although plays of one sort and another had been acted for many generations, no permanent playhouse was erected in England until 1576. In the 1570's the Lord Mayor and Aldermen of the City of London and the players were constantly at variance. As a result James Burbage, then the leader of the great Earl of Leicester's players, decided that he would erect a playhouse outside the jurisdiction of the Lord Mayor, where the players would no longer be hindered by the authorities. Accordingly in 1576 he built the Theatre in Shoreditch, at that time a suburb of London. The experiment was successful, and by 1592 there were two more playhouses in London, the Curtain (also in Shoreditch, and the Rose on the south bank of the river, near Southwark Cathedral.

Elizabethan players were accustomed to act on a variety of stages; in the great hall of a nobleman's house, or one of the Queen's palaces, in town halls and in yards, as well as their own theatre.

The public playhouse for which most of Shakespeare's plays were written was a small and intimate affair. The outside measurement of the Fortune Theatre, which was built in 1600 to rival the new Globe, was but eighty feet square. Playhouses were usually circular or octagonal, with three tiers of galleries looking down upon the yard or pit, which was open to the sky. The stage jutted out into the yard so that the actors came forward into the midst of their audience.

Over the stage there was a roof, and on either side doors by which the characters entered or disappeared. Over the back of the stage ran a gallery or upper stage which was used whenever an upper scene was needed, as when Romeo climbs up to Juliet's bedroom, or the citizens of Angiers address King John from the walls. The space beneath this upper stage was known as the tiring house; it was concealed from the audience by a curtain which would be drawn back to reveal an inner stage, for such scenes as the witches' cave in Macbeth, Prospero's cell or Juliet's tomb.

There was no general curtain concealing the whole stage, so that all scenes on the main stage began with an entrance and ended with an exit. Thus in tragedies the dead must be carried away. There was no scenery, and therefore no limit to the number of scenes, for a scene came to an end when the characters left the stage. When it was necessary for the exact locality of a scene to be known, then Shakespeare

THE GLOBE THEATRE

Wood-engraving by R. J. Beedham after a reconstruction by J. C. Adams

indicated it in the dialogue; otherwise a simple property or a garment was sufficient; a chair or stool showed an indoor scene, a man wearing riding boots was a messenger, a king wearing armour was on the battlefield, or the like. Such simplicity was on the whole an advantage; the spectator was not distracted by the setting and Shakespeare was able to use as many scenes as he wished. The action passed by very quickly: a play of 2500 lines of verse could be acted in two hours. Moreover, since the actor was so close to his audience, the slightest subtlety of voice and gesture was easily appreciated.

The company was a 'Fellowship of Players', who were all partners and sharers. There were usually ten to fifteen full members, with three or four boys, and some paid servants. Shakespeare had therefore to write for his team. The chief actor in the company was Richard Burbage, who first distinguished himself as Richard III; for him Shakespeare wrote his great tragic parts. An important member of the company was the clown or low comedian. From 1594 to 1600 the company's clown was Will Kemp; he was succeeded by Robert Armin. No women were allowed to appear on the stage, and all women's parts were taken by boys.

JULIUS CAESAR

The Tragedy of Julius Caesar was the first of Shakespeare's plays of Roman history. It was written, apparently, in the summer of 1599, and followed *As You Like it* and *Henry the Fifth*, which came out in the spring. In the many troubles and anxieties in the last five years of Queen Elizabeth's reign, books and especially plays on historical characters were very popular as being the nearest form of political discussion allowed at a time when it was dangerous to criticize the actions of authority. Early in 1599, a certain Dr John Hayward had published a history of the deposition of Richard the Second and the accession of Henry the Fourth. The book was considered so seditious that it was suppressed and the author subsequently imprisoned in the Tower. As a result of this scandal the Privy Council in June, 1599, issued an order suppressing books of satire, and commanding that thereafter no plays of English history should be printed unless allowed by a member of the Council. Plays of Roman history were not, however, illegal. The theme of *Julius Caesar* was apparently already in Shakespeare's mind when he was writing Henry V. Thus the Chorus before Act V appeals to the audience to imagine the citizens of London coming out to meet the King:

> 'Like to the senators of th' antique Rome,
> With the plebeians swarming at their heels,
> Go forth and fetch their conquering Caesar in:'

The play was being acted at the Globe Theatre in Southwark in the early autumn of 1599, when a German traveller, named Thomas Platter, visited England. Platter kept a journal of his travels in which he noted that

'After dinner on the 21st of September, at about two o'clock, I went with my companions over the water, and in the strewn roof-house [i.e., the playhouse with a thatched roof] saw the tragedy of the first Emperor Julius with at least fifteen characters very well acted. At the end of the comedy they danced according to their custom with extreme elegance. Two in men's clothes and two in women's gave this performance, in wonderful combination with each other.' [E. K. Chambers. *The Elizabethan Stage*, ii, 364 –5.]

The dance which Platter observed was the jig – a kind of crude ballet often performed at the end of a play.

Other references confirm the date 1599. Thus John Weever, in a poem on Sir John Oldcastle, called *The Mirror for Martyrs*, composed in 1599, though not published till 1601, wrote:

'The many-headed multitude were drawn
    By Brutus' speech, that Caesar was ambitious,
When eloquent Mark Antony had shown
    His virtues, who but Brutus then was vicious?'

Julius Caesar did not, however, please Ben Jonson. His two plays *Every Man in his Humour* and *Every Man out of his Humour* were acted by the Lord Chamberlain's Men in 1598 and 1599, but he quarrelled with the Company; and when he published *Every Man out of his Humour* in the spring of 1600 he added a few sneers at the Company, amongst them one at *Julius Caesar* – 'Reason long since is fled to animals, you know.' Years afterwards, when some of his jottings were published in 1641 under the title of *TIMBER or DISCOVERIES*, there appeared a critical paragraph on Shakespeare, in which he remarked, 'Many times he fell into those things, could not escape laughter: as when he said in the person of Caesar, one speaking to him; Caesar thou dost me wrong. He replied: Caesar did never wrong, but with just cause: and such like, which were ridiculous.' Probably Shakespeare altered the offending phrase, for in *Julius Caesar* the passage now reads:

'Know, Caesar doth not wrong, nor without cause
Will he be satisfied.' [*page* 64, *line* 12.]

Shakespeare took the story of the play from *Plutarch's Lives*. Plutarch was a Greek who died about A.D. 120. He wrote a series of parallel lives of famous Greeks and Romans, and, being interested less in history than in personality, he was more careful to record those little anecdotes and sayings which reveal character. The *Lives* were translated into French by Jacques Amyot, and from the French into English by Sir Thomas North in 1579. A second edition came out in 1595, published by Richard Field, who was also the printer of Shakespeare's *Venus and Adonis* and *Rape of Lucrece*. North's translation was very vivid, and Shakespeare made full use of it. Three of the *Lives* were used for the plot of *Julius Caesar* – Julius Caesar, Marcus Brutus, and Marcus Antonius.

The actual history of events between the return of Caesar to Rome, his murder on 15th March, 44 B.C., and the final battle of Philippi in 42 B.C., was very complex. Shakespeare vastly simplified the story into two main incidents: how Cassius and Brutus conspired to slay Caesar, and how Antony and young Octavius avenged the murder. The plot, as a whole, he constructed for himself, but he assembled the incidents from the various *Lives*. The Life of Caesar gave the episode of Antony offering the crown, the portents before the murder, the details of the murder, Cinna the poet, and the appearance of Caesar's ghost. In the Life of Brutus Shakespeare found full descriptions of the characters of Brutus and Cassius, how Cassius brought him into the conspiracy, the relationship between Brutus and his wife Portia, how Brutus spared Antony after the murder, how Antony stirred up the people. He found also Antony's opinion of Brutus, that

'of all them that had slain Caesar, there was none but Brutus only that was moved to do it, as thinking the act commendable of itself: but that all the other conspirators did conspire his death for some private malice or envy, that they otherwise did bear unto him.'

From the Life of Antonius came further details of the funeral speech, the proscriptions, the story of Cassius' death, and the funeral of Brutus.

Two quotations will give a fair sample of Shakespeare's material. Antony's speech over Caesar's body [Act III Scene 2] was thus described by Plutarch:

'... when Caesar's body was brought to the place where it should be buried, he made a funeral oration in commendation of Caesar, according to the ancient custom of praising noble men at their funerals. When he saw that the people were very glad and desirous also to hear Caesar spoken of, and his praises uttered, he mingled his oration with lamentable words; and by amplifying of matters did greatly move their hearts and affections unto pity and compassion. In fine, to conclude his oration, he unfolded before the whole assembly the bloody garments of the dead, thrust through in many places with their swords, and called the malefactors cruel and cursed murderers. With these words he put the people into such a fury, that they presently took Caesar's body, and burnt it in the market-place, with such tables and forms as they could get together. Then, when the fire was kindled, they took firebrands, and ran to the murderers' houses to set them on fire, and to make them come out to fight. Brutus, therefore, and his accomplices, for safety of their persons, were driven to fly the city.'

The scene of the quarrel between Brutus and Cassius [Act IV Scene 2] was made up of two incidents. In the first a disagreement between the two generals was ended by Phaeonius, a Cynic:

'This Phaeonius, at that time, in despite of the doorkeepers, came into the chamber, and with a certain scoffing and mocking gesture, which he counterfeited of purpose, he rehearsed the verses which old Nestor said in Homer:

> My lords, I pray you hearken both to me,
> For I have seen more years than such three.

Cassius fell a-laughing at him: but Brutus thrust him out of the chamber, and called him dog, and counterfeit Cynic. Howbeit his coming in brake their strife at that time, and so they left each other.' ...

'The next day after, Brutus, upon complaint of the Sardians, did condemn and note Lucius Pella for a defamed person, that had been a Praetor of the Romans, and whom Brutus had given charge unto: for that he was accused and convicted of robbery and pilfery in his office. This judgement much misliked Cassius, because he himself had secretly (not many days before) warned two of his friends, attainted and convicted of the like offences, and openly had cleared them: but yet he did not therefore leave to employ them in any manner of service as he did before. And therefore he greatly

reproved Brutus, for that he would show himself so straight
and severe, in such a time as was meeter to bear a little than
to take things at the worst. Brutus in contrary manner
answered, that he should remember the Ides of March, at
which time they slew Julius Caesar, who neither pilled nor
polled the country, but only was a favourer and suborner of
all them that did rob and spoil, by his countenance and
authority. And if there were any occasion whereby they
might honestly set aside justice and equity, they should have
had more reason to have suffered Caesar's friends to have
robbed and done what wrong and injury they had would
than to bear with their own men. "For then," said he, "they
could but have said we had been cowards, but now they
may accuse us of injustice, beside the pains we take, and the
danger we put ourselves into." And thus may we see what
Brutus' intent and purpose was.'

Julius Caesar was first published in the First Folio of 1623.
The text is excellently printed, with very few errors. In the
Folio the play is divided into Five Acts, but there are no
scene divisions; these have been added by later editors, and
are retained in this edition for convenience of reference.

The Folio text has its own peculiarities. It differs from
modern usage in several ways, particularly in spelling,
punctuation, and use of capitals. The modern custom is to
punctuate according to syntax; Elizabethan punctuation
was intended as guide for recitation or reading aloud.
Capital letters were used very freely. A modern editor is in
some difficulty; the 'accepted text' (which was the work of
editors of the eighteenth and nineteenth centuries) is some
way from Shakespeare's own text. On the other hand, to
reprint the Folio as it stands would annoy many readers who
are not scholars. The present text is a compromise. It follows

the Folio closely. Spelling is modernized, but the original arrangement and punctuation (which 'points' the text for reading aloud) have been left, except where they seemed definitely wrong. A few emendations generally accepted by editors have been kept. The reader who is used to an 'accepted text' may thus find certain unfamiliarities, but the text itself is nearer to that used in Shakespeare's own playhouse.

Julius Caesar

THE ACTORS' NAMES

JULIUS CAESAR
OCTAVIUS CAESAR
MARCUS ANTONIUS   } triumvirs after the death of
M. AEMILIUS LEPIDUS   }   Julius Caesar
CICERO   }
PUBLIUS   } Senators
POPILIUS LENA   }
MARCUS BRUTUS
CASSIUS
CASCA
TREBONIUS   } conspirators against Julius
LIGARIUS   }   Caesar
DECIUS BRUTUS
METELLUS CIMBER
CINNA
FLAVIUS and MARULLUS, Tribunes
ARTEMIDORUS
A Soothsayer
CINNA, a poet
Another Poet
LUCILIUS
TITINIUS
MESSALA   } friends to Brutus and Cassius
Young CATO
VOLUMNIUS
VARRO
CLITUS
CLAUDIUS   } servants to Brutus
STRATO
LUCIUS
DARDANIUS
PINDARUS, servant to Cassius
CALPURNIA, wife to Caesar
PORTIA, wife to Brutus

I. 1

Enter Flavius, Marullus, and certain Commoners
over the stage.

FLAVIUS: Hence: home you idle creatures, get you home:
  Is this a holiday? What, know you not
  (Being mechanical) you ought not walk
  Upon a labouring day, without the sign
  Of your profession? Speak, what trade art thou?

CARPENTER: Why sir, a carpenter.

MARULLUS: Where is thy leather apron, and thy rule?
  What dost thou with thy best apparel on?
  You sir, what trade are you?

COBBLER: Truly sir, in respect of a fine workman, I am but
  as you would say, a cobbler.

MARULLUS: But what trade art thou? Answer me directly.

COBBLER: A trade sir, that I hope I may use, with a
  safe conscience, which is indeed sir, a mender of bad
  soles.

FLAVIUS: What trade thou knave? Thou naughty knave,
  what trade?

COBBLER: Nay I beseech you sir, be not out with me: yet
  if you be out sir, I can mend you.

MARULLUS: What meanest thou by that? Mend me, thou
  saucy fellow?

COBBLER: Why sir, cobble you.

FLAVIUS: Thou art a cobbler, art thou?

COBBLER: Truly sir, all that I live by, is with the awl: I
  meddle with no tradesman's matters, nor women's matters; but withal I am indeed sir, a surgeon to old shoes:
  when they are in great danger, I recover them. As proper

men as ever trod upon neat's leather, have gone upon my
handiwork.

FLAVIUS: But wherefore art not in thy shop to-day?
Why dost thou lead these men about the streets?

COBBLER: Truly sir, to wear out their shoes, to get myself
into more work. But indeed sir, we make holiday to see
Caesar, and to rejoice in his Triumph.

MARULLUS: Wherefore rejoice?
What conquest brings he home?
What tributaries follow him to Rome,
To grace in captive bonds his chariot wheels?
You blocks, you stones, you worse than senseless things:
O you hard hearts, you cruel men of Rome,
Knew you not Pompey? Many a time and oft
Have you climb'd up to walls and battlements,
To towers and windows? Yea, to chimney tops,
Your infants in your arms, and there have sat
The live-long day, with patient expectation,
To see great Pompey pass the streets of Rome:
And when you saw his chariot but appear,
Have you not made an universal shout,
That Tiber trembled underneath her banks
To hear the replication of your sounds,
Made in her concave shores?
And do you now put on your best attire?
And do you now cull out a holyday?
And do you now strew flowers in his way,
That comes in triumph over Pompey's blood?
Be gone,
Run to your houses, fall upon your knees,
Pray to the Gods to intermit the plague
That needs must light on this ingratitude.

FLAVIUS: Go, go, good countrymen, and for this fault

Assemble all the poor men of your sort;
Draw them to Tiber banks, and weep your tears
Into the channel, till the lowest stream
Do kiss the most exalted shores of all.
                    Exeunt all the Commoners.
See where their basest metal be not mov'd,
They vanish tongue-tied in their guiltiness:
Go you down that way towards the Capitol,
This way will I: Disrobe the Images,
If you do find them deck'd with ceremonies.
MARULLUS: May we do so?
    You know it is the Feast of Lupercal.
FLAVIUS: It is no matter, let no Images
    Be hung with Caesar's trophies: I'll about,
    And drive away the vulgar from the streets;
    So do you too, where you perceive them thick.
    These growing feathers, pluck'd from Caesar's wing,
    Will make him fly an ordinary pitch,
    Who else would soar above the view of men,
    And keep us all in servile fearfulness.
                    Exeunt.

I. 2

*Enter Caesar, Antony for the course, Calpurnia, Portia,
Decius, Cicero, Brutus, Cassius, Casca, a Soothsayer:
after them Marullus and Flavius.*

CAESAR: Calpurnia.
CASCA: Peace ho, Caesar speaks.
CAESAR: Calpurnia.
CALPURNIA: Here my Lord.
CAESAR: Stand you directly in Antonius' way,
    When he doth run his course. Antonius.

ANTONY: Caesar, my Lord.

CAESAR: Forget not in your speed Antonius,
　To touch Calpurnia: for our Elders say,
　The barren touched in this holy chase,
　Shake off their sterile curse.

ANTONY: I shall remember,
　When Caesar says, Do this; it is perform'd.

CAESAR: Set on, and leave no ceremony out.

SOOTHSAYER: Caesar.

CAESAR: Ha? Who calls?

CASCA: Bid every noise be still: peace yet again.

CAESAR: Who is it in the press, that calls on me?
　I hear a tongue shriller than all the music
　Cry, Caesar: Speak, Caesar is turn'd to hear.

SOOTHSAYER: Beware the Ides of March.

CAESAR: What man is that?

BRUTUS: A Soothsayer bids you beware the Ides of March.

CAESAR: Set him before me, let me see his face.

CASSIUS: Fellow, come from the throng, look upon
　Caesar.

CAESAR: What say'st thou to me now? Speak once again.

SOOTHSAYER: Beware the Ides of March.

CAESAR: He is a dreamer, let us leave him: Pass.
　　　Sennet. Exeunt. Manent Brutus and Cassius.

CASSIUS: Will you go see the order of the course?

BRUTUS: Not I.

CASSIUS: I pray you do.

BRUTUS: I am not gamesome: I do lack some part
　Of that quick spirit that is in Antony:
　Let me not hinder Cassius your desires;
　I'll leave you.

CASSIUS: Brutus, I do observe you now of late:
　I have not from your eyes, that gentleness

And show of love, as I was wont to have:
You bear too stubborn, and too strange a hand
Over your friend, that loves you.

BRUTUS: Cassius,
Be not deceiv'd: If I have veil'd my look,
I turn the trouble of my countenance
Merely upon myself. Vexed I am
Of late, with passions of some difference,
Conceptions only proper to myself,
Which give some soil (perhaps) to my behaviours:
But let not therefore my good friends be griev'd
(Among which number Cassius be you one)
Nor construe any further my neglect,
Than that poor Brutus with himself at war,
Forgets the shows of love to other men.

CASSIUS: Then Brutus, I have much mistook your passion,
By means whereof, this breast of mine hath buried
Thoughts of great value, worthy cogitations.
Tell me good Brutus, Can you see your face?

BRUTUS: No Cassius:
For the eye sees not itself but by reflection,
By some other things.

CASSIUS: 'Tis just,
And it is very much lamented Brutus,
That you have no such mirrors, as will turn
Your hidden worthiness into your eye,
That you might see your shadow:
I have heard,
Where many of the best respect in Rome
(Except immortal Caesar), speaking of Brutus,
And groaning underneath this Age's yoke,
Have wish'd, that noble Brutus had his eyes.

BRUTUS: Into what dangers, would you lead me Cassius?

That you would have me seek into myself,
For that which is not in me?
CASSIUS: Therefore good Brutus, be prepar'd to hear:
  And since you know, you cannot see yourself
  So well as by reflection; I your glass,
  Will modestly discover to yourself
  That of yourself, which you yet know not of.
  And be not jealous on me, gentle Brutus:
  Were I a common laughter, or did use
  To stale with ordinary oaths my love
  To every new protester: if you know,
  That I do fawn on men, and hug them hard,
  And after scandal them: Or if you know,
  That I profess myself in banqueting
  To all the rout, then hold me dangerous.
            Flourish, and shout.
BRUTUS: What means this shouting?
  I do fear, the people choose Caesar
  For their King.
CASSIUS: Ay, do you fear it?
  Then must I think you would not have it so.
BRUTUS: I would not Cassius, yet I love him well:
  But wherefore do you hold me here so long?
  What is it, that you would impart to me?
  If it be aught toward the general good,
  Set Honour in one eye, and Death i' th' other,
  And I will look on both indifferently:
  For let the Gods so speed me, as I love
  The name of Honour, more than I fear death.
CASSIUS: I know that virtue to be in you Brutus,
  As well as I do know your outward favour.
  Well, Honour is the subject of my story:
  I cannot tell, what you and other men

Think of this life: But for my single self,
I had as lief not be, as live to be
In awe of such a Thing, as I myself.
I was born free as Caesar, so were you,
We both have fed as well, and we can both
Endure the winter's cold, as well as he.
For once, upon a raw and gusty day,
The troubled Tiber, chafing with her shores,
Caesar said to me, Dar'st thou Cassius now
Leap in with me into this angry flood,
And swim to yonder point? Upon the word,
Accoutred as I was, I plunged in,
And bade him follow: so indeed he did.
The torrent roar'd, and we did buffet it
With lusty sinews, throwing it aside,
And stemming it with hearts of controversy.
But ere we could arrive the point propos'd,
Caesar cried, Help me Cassius, or I sink.
I (as Aeneas, our great ancestor,
Did from the flames of Troy, upon his shoulder
The old Anchises bear) so, from the waves of Tiber
Did I the tired Caesar: and this Man,
Is now become a God, and Cassius is
A wretched creature, and must bend his body,
If Caesar carelessly but nod on him.
He had a fever when he was in Spain,
And when the fit was on him, I did mark
How he did shake: 'Tis true, this God did shake,
His coward lips did from their colour fly,
And that same eye, whose bend doth awe the World,
Did lose his lustre: I did hear him groan:
Ay, and that tongue of his, that bad the Romans
Mark him, and write his speeches in their books,

Alas, it cried, Give me some drink Titinius,
As a sick girl: ye Gods, it doth amaze me,
A man of such a feeble temper should
So get the start of the majestic world,
And bear the palm alone.

              Shout.   *Flourish.*

BRUTUS: Another general shout?
  I do believe, that these applauses are
  For some new honours, that are heap'd on Caesar.
CASSIUS: Why man, he doth bestride the narrow world
  Like a Colossus, and we petty men
  Walk under his huge legs, and peep about
  To find ourselves dishonourable graves.
  Men at some time, are masters of their fates.
  The fault (dear Brutus) is not in our Stars,
  But in ourselves, that we are underlings.
  Brutus and Caesar: What should be in that Caesar?
  Why should that name be sounded more than yours?
  Write them together: yours, is as fair a name:
  Sound them, it doth become the mouth as well:
  Weigh them, it is as heavy: Conjure with 'em,
  Brutus will start a spirit as soon as Caesar.
  Now in the names of all the Gods at once,
  Upon what meat doth this our Caesar feed,
  That he is grown so great? Age, thou art sham'd.
  Rome, thou hast lost the breed of Noble Bloods.
  When went there by an Age, since the great Flood,
  But it was fam'd with more than with one man?
  When could they say (till now) that talk'd of Rome,
  That her wide walls encompass'd but one man?
  Now is it Rome indeed, and room enough,
  When there is in it but one only man.
  O! you and I, have heard our Fathers say,

There was a Brutus once, that would have brook'd
Th' eternal Devil to keep his state in Rome,
As easily as a King.
BRUTUS: That you do love me, I am nothing jealous:
What you would work me to, I have some aim:
How I have thought of this, and of these times
I shall recount hereafter. For this present,
I would not (so with love I might entreat you)
Be any further mov'd: What you have said,
I will consider: what you have to say
I will with patience hear, and find a time
Both meet to hear, and answer such high things.
Till then, my noble friend, chew upon this:
Brutus had rather be a villager,
Than to repute himself a son of Rome
Under these hard conditions, as this time
Is like to lay upon us.
CASSIUS: I am glad that my weak words
Have struck but thus much show of fire from Brutus.
Enter Caesar and his train.
BRUTUS: The games are done,
And Caesar is returning.
CASSIUS: As they pass by,
Pluck Casca by the sleeve,
And he will (after his sour fashion) tell you
What hath proceeded worthy note today.
BRUTUS: I will do so: but look you Cassius,
The angry spot doth glow on Caesar's brow,
And all the rest, look like a chidden train;
Calpurnia's cheek is pale, and Cicero
Looks with such ferret, and such fiery eyes
As we have seen him in the Capitol
Being cross'd in conference, by some Senators.

CASSIUS: Casca will tell us what the matter is.

CAESAR: Antonius.

ANTONY: Caesar.

CAESAR: Let me have men about me, that are fat,
Sleek-headed men, and such as sleep o' nights:
Yond Cassius has a lean and hungry look,
He thinks too much: such men are dangerous.

ANTONY: Fear him not Caesar, he's not dangerous,
He is a noble Roman, and well given.

CAESAR: Would he were fatter; But I fear him not:
Yet if my name were liable to fear,
I do not know the man I should avoid
So soon as that spare Cassius. He reads much,
He is a great observer, and he looks
Quite through the deeds of men. He loves no plays,
As thou dost Antony: he hears no music;
Seldom he smiles, and smiles in such a sort
As if he mock'd himself, and scorn'd his spirit
That could be mov'd to smile at any thing.
Such men as he, be never at heart's ease,
Whiles they behold a greater than themselves,
And therefore are they very dangerous.
I rather tell thee what is to be fear'd,
Than what I fear: for always I am Caesar.
Come on my right hand, for this ear is deaf,
And tell me truly, what thou think'st of him.

Sennet. Exeunt Caesar and his Train, all but Casca.

CASCA: You pull'd me by the cloak, would you speak with
me?

BRUTUS: Ay Casca, tell us what hath chanc'd today
That Caesar looks so sad.

CASCA: Why you were with him, were you not?

BRUTUS: I should not then ask Casca what had chanc'd.

CASCA: Why there was a Crown offer'd him; and being offer'd him, he put it by with the back of his hand thus, and then the people fell a-shouting.

BRUTUS: What was the second noise for?

CASCA: Why for that too.

CASSIUS: They shouted thrice: what was the last cry for?

CASCA: Why for that too.

BRUTUS: Was the Crown offer'd him thrice?

CASCA: Ay marry was't, and he put it by thrice, every time gentler than other; and at every putting by, mine honest neighbours shouted.

CASSIUS: Who offer'd him the Crown?

CASCA: Why Antony.

BRUTUS: Tell us the manner of it, gentle Casca.

CASCA: I can as well be hang'd as tell the manner of it: It was mere foolery, I did not mark it. I saw Mark Antony offer him a Crown, yet 'twas not a Crown neither, 'twas one of these Coronets: and as I told you, he put it by once: but for all that, to my thinking, he would fain have had it. Then he offered it to him again: then he put it by again: but to my thinking, he was very loath to lay his fingers off it. And then he offered it the third time; he put it the third time by, and still as he refus'd it, the rabblement hooted, and clapp'd their chopt hands, and threw up their sweaty night-caps, and uttered such a deal of stinking breath, because Caesar refus'd the crown, that it had (almost) choked Caesar: for he swounded, and fell down at it: And for mine own part, I durst not laugh, for fear of opening my lips, and receiving the bad air.

CASSIUS: But soft I pray you: what, did Caesar swound?

CASCA: He fell down in the Market-place, and foam'd at mouth, and was speechless.

BRUTUS: 'Tis very like he hath the falling sickness.

CASSIUS: No, Caesar hath it not: but you, and I,
And honest Casca, we have the falling sickness.

CASCA: I know not what you mean by that, but I am sure
Caesar fell down. If the tag-rag people did not clap him,
and hiss him, according as he pleas'd, and displeas'd them,
as they use to do the Players in the Theatre, I am no true
man.

BRUTUS: What said he, when he came unto himself?

CASCA: Marry, before he fell down, when he perceiv'd the
common herd was glad he refus'd the Crown, he pluck'd
me ope his doublet, and offer'd them his throat to cut:
and I had been a man of any occupation, if I would not
have taken him at a word, I would I might go to Hell
among the rogues, and so he fell. When he came to himself again, he said, If he had done, or said any thing
amiss, he desir'd their Worships to think it was his in-
firmity. Three or four wenches where I stood, cried,
Alas good soul, and forgave him with all their hearts:
But there's no heed to be taken of them; if Caesar had
stabb'd their Mothers, they would have done no less.

BRUTUS: And after that, he came thus sad away.

CASCA: Ay.

CASSIUS: Did Cicero say anything?

CASCA: Ay, he spoke Greek.

CASSIUS: To what effect?

CASCA: Nay, and I tell you that, I'll ne'er look you i' th'
face again. But those that understood him, smil'd at one
another, and shook their heads: but for mine own part, it
was Greek to me. I could tell you more news too:
Marullus and Flavius, for pulling scarfs off Caesar's
Images, are put to silence. Fare you well. There was more
foolery yet, if I could remember it.

CASSIUS: Will you sup with me tonight, Casca?

CASCA: No, I am promis'd forth.

CASSIUS: Will you dine with me tomorrow?

CASCA: Ay, if I be alive, and your mind hold, and your
dinner worth the eating.

CASSIUS: Good, I will expect you.

CASCA: Do so: farewell both.

Exit.

BRUTUS: What a blunt fellow is this grown to be?
He was quick mettle, when he went to school.

CASSIUS: So is he now, in execution
Of any bold, or noble enterprise,
However he puts on this tardy form:
This rudeness is a sauce to his good wit,
Which gives men stomach to digest his words
With better appetite.

BRUTUS: And so it is:
For this time I will leave you:
Tomorrow, if you please to speak with me,
I will come home to you: or if you will,
Come home to me, and I will wait for you.

CASSIUS: I will do so: till then, think of the world.

Exit Brutus.

Well Brutus, thou art noble: yet I see,
Thy honourable metal may be wrought
From that it is dispos'd: therefore it is meet,
That noble minds keep ever with their likes:
For who so firm, that cannot be seduc'd?
Caesar doth bear me hard, but he loves Brutus.
If I were Brutus now, and he were Cassius,
He should not humour me. I will this night,
In several hands, in at his windows throw,
As if they came from several citizens,
Writings, all tending to the great opinion

That Rome holds of his name: wherein obscurely
Caesar's ambition shall be glanced at.
And after this, let Caesar seat him sure,
For we will shake him, or worse days endure.

Exit.

I. 3

Thunder and lightning. Enter Casca, and Cicero.

CICERO: Good even, Casca: brought you Caesar home?
Why are you breathless, and why stare you so?

CASCA: Are not you mov'd, when all the sway of Earth
Shakes, like a thing unfirm? O Cicero,
I have seen tempests, when the scolding winds
Have riv'd the knotty oaks, and I have seen
Th' ambitious Ocean swell, and rage, and foam,
To be exalted with the threatening clouds:
But never till tonight, never till now,
Did I go through a tempest-dropping-fire.
Either there is a civil strife in Heaven,
Or else the World, too saucy with the Gods,
Incenses them to send destruction.

CICERO: Why, saw you any thing more wonderful?

CASCA: A common slave, you know him well by sight,
Held up his left hand, which did flame and burn
Like twenty torches join'd; and yet his hand,
Not sensible of fire, remain'd unscorch'd.
Besides, I ha' not since put up my sword,
Against the Capitol I met a lion,
Who glaz'd upon me, and went surly by,
Without annoying me. And there were drawn
Upon a heap, a hundred ghastly women,
Transformed with their fear, who swore, they saw

Men, all in fire, walk up and down the streets.
And yesterday the Bird of Night did sit,
Even at noon-day, upon the Market-place,
Hooting, and shrieking. When these Prodigies
Do so conjointly meet, let not men say,
These are their reasons, they are natural:
For I believe, they are portentous things
Unto the climate, that they point upon.

CICERO: Indeed, it is a strange disposed time:
　But men may construe things after their fashion,
　Clean from the purpose of the things themselves.
　Comes Caesar to the Capitol tomorrow?

CASCA: He doth: for he did bid Antonius
　Send word to you, he would be there tomorrow.

CICERO: Good night then, Casca:
　This disturbed sky is not to walk in.

CASCA: Farewell Cicero.

Exit Cicero.
Enter Cassius.

CASSIUS: Who's there?

CASCA: A Roman.

CASSIUS: Casca, by your voice.

CASCA: Your ear is good.
　Cassius, what night is this?

CASSIUS: A very pleasing night to honest men.

CASCA: Who ever knew the Heavens menace so?

CASSIUS: Those that have known the Earth so full of
　faults.
　For my part, I have walk'd about the streets,
　Submitting me unto the perilous night;
　And thus unbraced, Casca, as you see,
　Have bar'd my bosom to the thunder-stone:
　And when the cross blue lightning seem'd to open

The breast of Heaven, I did present myself
Even in the aim, and very flash of it.

CASCA: But wherefore did you so much tempt the
Heavens?
It is the part of men, to fear and tremble,
When the most mighty Gods, by tokens send
Such dreadful Heralds, to astonish us.

CASSIUS: You are dull, Casca:
And those sparks of life, that should be in a Roman,
You do want, or else you use not.
You look pale, and gaze, and put on fear,
And cast yourself in wonder,
To see the strange impatience of the Heavens:
But if you would consider the true cause,
Why all these fires, why all these gliding ghosts,
Why birds and beasts, from quality and kind,
Why old men, fools, and children calculate,
Why all these things change from their ordinance,
Their natures, and pre-formed faculties,
To monstrous quality; why you shall find,
That Heaven hath infus'd them with these spirits,
To make them instruments of fear, and warning,
Unto some monstrous state.
Now could I (Casca) name to thee a man,
Most like this dreadful night,
That thunders, lightens, opens graves, and roars,
As doth the lion in the Capitol:
A man no mightier than thyself, or me,
In personal action; yet prodigious grown,
And fearful, as these strange eruptions are.

CASCA: 'Tis Caesar that you mean:
Is it not, Cassius?

CASSIUS: Let it be who it is: for Romans now

Have thews, and limbs, like to their Ancestors:
But, woe the while, our Fathers' minds are dead,
And we are govern'd with our Mothers' spirits,
Our yoke, and sufferance, show us womanish.

CASCA: Indeed, they say, the Senators tomorrow
Mean to establish Caesar as a King:
And he shall wear his Crown by sea, and land,
In every place, save here in Italy.

CASSIUS: I know where I will wear this dagger then;
Cassius from bondage will deliver Cassius:
Therein, ye Gods, you make the weak most strong;
Therein, ye Gods, you Tyrants do defeat.
Nor stony tower, nor walls of beaten brass,
Nor air-less dungeon, nor strong links of iron,
Can be retentive to the strength of spirit:
But Life being weary of these worldly bars,
Never lacks power to dismiss itself.
If I know this, know all the World besides,
That part of tyranny that I do bear,
I can shake off at pleasure.

Thunder still.

CASCA: So can I:
So every bond-man in his own hand bears
The power to cancel his captivity.

CASSIUS: And why should Caesar be a Tyrant then?
Poor man, I know he would not be a wolf,
But that he sees the Romans are but sheep:
He were no lion, were not Romans hinds.
Those that with haste will make a mighty fire,
Begin it with weak straws. What trash is Rome?
What rubbish, and what offal? when it serves
For the base matter, to illuminate
So vile a thing as Caesar. But oh Grief,

Where hast thou led me? I (perhaps) speak this
Before a willing bond-man: then I know
My answer must be made. But I am arm'd,
And dangers are to me indifferent.

CASCA: You speak to Casca, and to such a man,
That is no fleering tell-tale. Hold, my hand:
Be factious for redress of all these griefs,
And I will set this foot of mine as far,
As who goes farthest.

CASSIUS: There's a bargain made.
Now know you, Casca, I have mov'd already
Some certain of the noblest minded Romans
To undergo, with me, an enterprise,
Of honourable dangerous consequence;
And I do know by this, they stay for me
In Pompey's Porch: for now this fearful night,
There is no stir, or walking in the streets;
And the complexion of the element
In favour's, like the work we have in hand,
Most bloody, fiery, and most terrible.

Enter Cinna.

CASCA: Stand close awhile, for here comes one in
haste.

CASSIUS: 'Tis Cinna, I do know him by his gait,
He is a friend. Cinna, where haste you so?

CINNA: To find out you: Who's that, Metellus Cimber?

CASSIUS: No, it is Casca, one incorporate
To our attempts. Am I not stay'd for, Cinna?

CINNA: I am glad on't.
What a fearful night is this?
There's two or three of us have seen strange sights.

CASSIUS: Am I not stay'd for? tell me.

CINNA: Yes, you are. O Cassius,

If you could but win the noble Brutus
To our party –
CASSIUS: Be you content. Good Cinna, take this paper,
And look you lay it in the Praetor's chair,
Where Brutus may but find it: and throw this
In at his window; set this up with wax
Upon old Brutus' statue: all this done,
Repair to Pompey's Porch, where you shall find us.
Is Decius Brutus and Trebonius there?
CINNA: All, but Metellus Cimber, and he's gone
To seek you at your house. Well, I will hie,
And so bestow these papers as you bad me.
CASSIUS: That done, repair to Pompey's Theatre.
Exit Cinna.
Come Casca, you and I will yet, ere day,
See Brutus at his house: three parts of him
Is ours already, and the man entire
Upon the next encounter, yields him ours.
CASCA: O, he sits high in all the People's hearts:
And that which would appear offence in us,
His countenance, like richest alchemy,
Will change to virtue, and to worthiness.
CASSIUS: Him, and his worth, and our great need of him,
You have right well conceited: let us go,
For it is after midnight, and ere day,
We will awake him, and be sure of him.
Exeunt.

II. 1

Enter Brutus in his orchard.

BRUTUS: What Lucius, ho?
I cannot, by the progress of the stars,
Give guess how near to day – Lucius, I say?
I would it were my fault to sleep so soundly.
When Lucius, when? awake, I say: what Lucius?

Enter Lucius.

LUCIUS: Call'd you, my Lord?

BRUTUS: Get me a taper in my study, Lucius:
When it is lighted, come and call me here.

LUCIUS: I will, my Lord.

Exit.

BRUTUS: It must be by his death: and for my part,
I know no personal cause, to spurn at him,
But for the general. He would be crown'd:
How that might change his nature, there's the question?
It is the bright day, that brings forth the adder,
And that craves wary walking: Crown him that,
And then I grant we put a sting in him,
That at his will he may do danger with.
Th' abuse of Greatness, is, when it disjoins
Remorse from Power: And to speak truth of Caesar,
I have not known, when his affections sway'd
More than his reason. But 'tis a common proof,
That Lowliness is young Ambition's ladder,
Whereto the climber upward turns his face:
But when he once attains the upmost round,
He then unto the ladder turns his back,
Looks in the clouds, scorning the base degrees
By which he did ascend: so Caesar may;

Then lest he may, prevent. And since the quarrel
Will bear no colour, for the thing he is,
Fashion it thus; that what he is, augmented,
Would run to these, and these extremities:
And therefore think him as a serpent's egg,
Which hatch'd, would as his kind grow mischievous;
And kill him in the shell.

Enter Lucius.

LUCIUS: The taper burneth in your closet, sir:
Searching the window for a flint, I found
This paper, thus seal'd up, and I am sure
It did not lie there when I went to bed.

Gives him the letter.

BRUTUS: Get you to bed again, it is not day:
Is not tomorrow (Boy) the Ides of March?

LUCIUS: I know not, sir.

BRUTUS: Look in the Calendar, and bring me word.

LUCIUS: I will, sir.

Exit.

BRUTUS: The exhalations, whizzing in the air,
Give so much light, that I may read by them.

Opens the letter, and reads.

Brutus thou sleep'st; awake, and see thyself:
Shall Rome, &c. Speak, strike, redress.
Brutus, thou sleep'st: awake.
Such instigations have been often dropp'd,
Where I have took them up:
Shall Rome, &c. Thus must I piece it out:
Shall Rome stand under one man's awe? What Rome?
My Ancestors did from the streets of Rome
The Tarquin drive, when he was call'd a King.
Speak, strike, redress. Am I entreated
To speak, and strike? O Rome, I make thee promise,

If the redress will follow, thou receivest
Thy full petition at the hand of Brutus.
                    Enter Lucius.
LUCIUS: Sir, March is wasted fourteen days.
                    Knock within.
BRUTUS: 'Tis good. Go to the gate, somebody knocks:
                    Exit Lucius.
Since Cassius first did whet me against Caesar,
I have not slept.
Between the acting of a dreadful thing,
And the first motion, all the interim is
Like a phantasma, or a hideous dream:
The Genius, and the mortal instruments
Are then in council; and the state of man,
Like to a little Kingdom, suffers then
The nature of an Insurrection.
                    Enter Lucius.
LUCIUS: Sir, 'tis your brother Cassius at the door,
Who doth desire to see you.
BRUTUS: Is he alone?
LUCIUS: No, sir, there are moe with him.
BRUTUS: Do you know them?
LUCIUS: No, sir, their hats are pluck'd about their ears,
And half their faces buried in their cloaks,
That by no means I may discover them,
By any mark of favour.
BRUTUS: Let 'em enter:
                    Exit Lucius.
They are the faction. O Conspiracy,
Sham'st thou to show thy dang'rous brow by night,
When evils are most free? O then, by day
Where wilt thou find a cavern dark enough,
To mask thy monstrous visage? Seek none Conspiracy,

Hide it in smiles, and affability:
For if thou path thy native semblance on,
Not Erebus itself were dim enough,
To hide thee from prevention.
Enter the Conspirators, Cassius, Casca, Decius, Cinna,
Metellus, and Trebonius.

CASSIUS: I think we are too bold upon your rest:
Good morrow Brutus, do we trouble you?

BRUTUS: I have been up this hour, awake all night:
Know I these men, that come along with you?

CASSIUS: Yes, every man of them; and no man here
But honours you: and every one doth wish,
You had but that opinion of yourself,
Which every noble Roman bears of you.
This is Trebonius.

BRUTUS: He is welcome hither.

CASSIUS: This, Decius Brutus.

BRUTUS: He is welcome too.

CASSIUS: This, Casca; this, Cinna; and this, Metellus
Cimber.

BRUTUS: They are all welcome.
What watchful cares do interpose themselves
Betwixt your eyes, and night?

CASSIUS: Shall I entreat a word?
They whisper.

DECIUS: Here lies the East: doth not the day break here?

CASCA: No.

CINNA: O pardon, sir, it doth; and yon grey lines,
That fret the clouds, are messengers of Day.

CASCA: You shall confess, that you are both deceiv'd:
Here, as I point my sword, the Sun arises,
Which is a great way growing on the South,
Weighing the youthful season of the year.

Some two months hence, up higher toward the North
He first presents his fire, and the high East
Stands as the Capitol, directly here.
BRUTUS: Give me your hands all over, one by one.
CASSIUS: And let us swear our resolution.
BRUTUS: No, not an oath: if not the face of men,
　The sufferance of our souls, the time's abuse;
　If these be motives weak, break off betimes,
　And every man hence, to his idle bed:
　So let high-sighted Tyranny range on,
　Till each man drop by lottery. But if these
　(As I am sure they do) bear fire enough
　To kindle cowards, and to steel with valour
　The melting spirits of women, then countrymen,
　What need we any spur, but our own cause
　To prick us to redress? What other bond,
　Than secret Romans, that have spoke the word,
　And will not palter? And what other oath,
　Than Honesty to Honesty engag'd,
　That this shall be, or we will fall for it.
　Swear priests and cowards, and men cautelous
　Old feeble carrions, and such suffering souls
　That welcome wrongs: Unto bad causes, swear
　Such creatures as men doubt; but do not stain
　The even virtue of our enterprise,
　Nor th' insuppressive mettle of our spirits,
　To think, that or our cause, or our performance
　Did need an oath. When every drop of blood
　That every Roman bears, and nobly bears
　Is guilty of a several bastardy,
　If he do break the smallest particle
　Of any promise that hath pass'd from him.
CASSIUS: But what of Cicero? Shall we sound him?

I think he will stand very strong with us.

CASCA: Let us not leave him out.

CINNA: No, by no means.

METELLUS: O let us have him, for his silver hairs
Will purchase us a good opinion:
And buy men's voices, to commend our deeds:
It shall be said, his judgement rul'd our hands,
Our youths, and wildness, shall no whit appear,
But all be buried in his gravity.

BRUTUS: O name him not; let us not break with him,
For he will never follow any thing
That other men begin.

CASSIUS: Then leave him out.

CASCA: Indeed, he is not fit.

DECIUS: Shall no man else be touch'd, but only Caesar?

CASSIUS: Decius well urg'd: I think it is not meet,
Mark Antony, so well belov'd of Caesar,
Should outlive Caesar, we shall find of him
A shrewd contriver. And you know, his means
If he improve them, may well stretch so far
As to annoy us all: which to prevent,
Let Antony and Caesar fall together.

BRUTUS: Our course will seem too bloody, Caius Cassius,
To cut the head off, and then hack the limbs:
Like Wrath in death, and Envy afterwards:
For Antony, is but a limb of Caesar.
Let us be sacrificers, but not butchers Caius:
We all stand up against the spirit of Caesar,
And in the spirit of men, there is no blood:
O that we then could come by Caesar's spirit,
And not dismember Caesar! But (alas)
Caesar must bleed for it. And gentle friends,
Let's kill him boldly, but not wrathfully:

Let's carve him, as a dish fit for the Gods,
Not hew him as a carcass fit for hounds:
And let our hearts, as subtle Masters do,
Stir up their servants to an act of rage,
And after seem to chide 'em. This shall make
Our purpose necessary, and not envious.
Which so appearing to the common eyes,
We shall be call'd purgers, not murderers.
And for Mark Antony, think not of him:
For he can do no more than Caesar's arm,
When Caesar's head is off.

CASSIUS: Yet I fear him,
For in the ingrafted love he bears to Caesar.

BRUTUS: Alas, good Cassius, do not think of him:
If he love Caesar, all that he can do
Is to himself; take thought, and die for Caesar,
And that were much he should: for he is given
To sports, to wildness, and much company.

TREBONIUS: There is no fear in him; let him not die,
For he will live, and laugh at this hereafter.

Clock strikes.

BRUTUS: Peace, count the clock.

CASSIUS: The clock hath stricken three.

TREBONIUS: 'Tis time to part.

CASSIUS: But it is doubtful yet,
Whether Caesar will come forth today, or no:
For he is superstitious grown of late,
Quite from the main opinion he held once,
Of fantasy, of dreams, and ceremonies:
It may be, these apparent prodigies,
The unaccustom'd terror of this night,
And the persuasion of his Augurers,
May hold him from the Capitol today.

DECIUS: Never fear that: If he be so resolv'd,
  I can o'ersway him: For he loves to hear,
  That unicorns may be betray'd with trees,
  And bears with glasses, elephants with holes,
  Lions with toils, and men with flatterers.
  But, when I tell him, he hates flatterers,
  He says, he does; being then most flattered.
  Let me work:
  For I can give his humour the true bent;
  And I will bring him to the Capitol.

CASSIUS: Nay, we will all of us, be there to fetch him.

BRUTUS: By the eighth hour, is that the uttermost?

CINNA: Be that the uttermost, and fail not then.

METELLUS: Caius Ligarius doth bear Caesar hard,
  Who rated him for speaking well of Pompey;
  I wonder none of you have thought of him.

BRUTUS: Now good Metellus go along by him:
  He loves me well, and I have given him reasons,
  Send him but hither, and I'll fashion him.

CASSIUS: The morning comes upon's:
  We'll leave you Brutus,
  And friends disperse yourselves; but all remember
  What you have said, and show yourselves true Romans.

BRUTUS: Good Gentlemen, look fresh and merrily,
  Let not our looks put on our purposes,
  But bear it as our Roman Actors do,
  With untir'd spirits, and formal constancy,
  And so good morrow to you every one.

Exeunt.
Manet Brutus.

Boy: Lucius: Fast asleep? It is no matter,
  Enjoy the honey-heavy dew of slumber:
  Thou hast no figures, nor no fantasies,

Which busy care draws, in the brains of men;
Therefore thou sleep'st so sound.

Enter Portia.

PORTIA: Brutus, my Lord.

BRUTUS: Portia: What mean you? wherefore rise you
now?
It is not for your health, thus to commit
Your weak condition, to the raw cold morning.

PORTIA: Nor for yours neither. Y'have ungently Brutus
Stole from my bed: and yesternight at supper
You suddenly arose, and walk'd about,
Musing, and sighing, with your arms across:
And when I ask'd you what the matter was,
You star'd upon me, with ungentle looks.
I urg'd you further, then you scratch'd your head,
And too impatiently stamp'd with your foot:
Yet I insisted, yet you answer'd not,
But with an angry wafture of your hand
Gave sign for me to leave you: So I did,
Fearing to strengthen that impatience
Which seem'd too much enkindled; and withal,
Hoping it was but an effect of Humour,
Which sometime hath his hour with every man.
It will not let you eat, nor talk, nor sleep;
And could it work so much upon your shape,
As it hath much prevail'd on your condition,
I should not know you Brutus. Dear my Lord,
Make me acquainted with your cause of grief.

BRUTUS: I am not well in health, and that is all.

PORTIA: Brutus is wise, and were he not in health,
He would embrace the means to come by it.

BRUTUS: Why so I do: good Portia go to bed.

PORTIA: Is Brutus sick? And is it physical

To walk unbraced, and suck up the humours
Of the dank morning? What, is Brutus sick?
And will he steal out of his wholesome bed
To dare the vile contagion of the Night?
And tempt the rheumy, and unpurged air,
To add unto his sickness? No my Brutus,
You have some sick offence within your mind,
Which by the right and virtue of my place
I ought to know of: And upon my knees,
I charm you, by my once commended beauty,
By all your vows of Love, and that great vow
Which did incorporate and make us one,
That you unfold to me, yourself, your half,
Why you are heavy: and what men tonight
Have had resort to you: for here have been
Some six or seven, who did hide their faces
Even from darkness.

BRUTUS: Kneel not gentle Portia.

PORTIA: I should not need, if you were gentle Brutus.
Within the Bond of Marriage, tell me Brutus,
Is it excepted, I should know no secrets
That appertain to you? Am I yourself,
But as it were in sort, or limitation?
To keep with you at meals, comfort your bed,
And talk to you sometimes? Dwell I but in the suburbs
Of your good pleasure? If it be no more,
Portia is Brutus' Harlot, not his Wife.

BRUTUS: You are my true and honourable Wife,
As dear to me, as are the ruddy drops
That visit my sad heart.

PORTIA: If this were true, then should I know this secret.
I grant I am a woman; but withal,
A woman that Lord Brutus took to wife:

I grant I am a woman; but withal,
A woman well-reputed: Cato's daughter.
Think you, I am no stronger than my sex
Being so father'd, and so husbanded?
Tell me your counsels, I will not disclose 'em:
I have made strong proof of my constancy,
Giving myself a voluntary wound
Here, in the thigh: Can I bear that with patience,
And not my husband's secrets?

BRUTUS: O ye gods!
 Render me worthy of this noble wife.   *Knock.*
 Hark, hark, one knocks: Portia go in awhile,
 And by and by thy bosom shall partake
 The secrets of my heart.
 All my engagements, I will construe to thee,
 All the charactery of my sad brows:
 Leave me with haste.

Exit Portia.
Enter Lucius and Ligarius.

 Lucius, who's that knocks?

LUCIUS: Here is a sick man that would speak with you.

BRUTUS: Caius Ligarius, that Metellus spake of.
 Boy, stand aside. Caius Ligarius, how?

LIGARIUS: Vouchsafe good morrow from a feeble tongue.

BRUTUS: O what a time have you chose out brave Caius
 To wear a kerchief? Would you were not sick.

LIGARIUS: I am not sick, if Brutus have in hand
 Any exploit worthy the name of honour.

BRUTUS: Such an exploit have I in hand Ligarius,
 Had you a healthful care to hear of it.

LIGARIUS: By all the gods that Romans bow before,
 I here discard my sickness. Soul of Rome,
 Brave son, deriv'd from honourable loins,

Thou like an exorcist, hast conjur'd up
My mortified spirit. Now bid me run,
And I will strive with things impossible,
Yea, get the better of them. What's to do?
BRUTUS: A piece of work,
That will make sick men whole.
LIGARIUS: But are not some whole, that we must make
   sick?
BRUTUS: That must we also. What it is my Caius,
I shall unfold to thee, as we are going,
To whom it must be done.
LIGARIUS: Set on your foot,
And with a heart new-fir'd, I follow you,
To do I know not what: but it sufficeth
That Brutus leads me on.   *Thunder.*
BRUTUS: Follow me then.
                    Exeunt.

II.2

Thunder and lightning. Enter Julius Caesar in his
night-gown.
CAESAR: Nor Heaven, nor Earth,
Have been at peace tonight:
Thrice hath Calpurnia, in her sleep cried out,
Help, ho: They murther Caesar. Who's within?
                    Enter a Servant.
SERVANT: My Lord.
CAESAR: Go bid the Priests do present sacrifice,
And bring me their opinions of success.
SERVANT: I will my Lord.
                    Exit.
                    Enter Calpurnia.

CALPURNIA: What mean you Caesar? Think you to walk
   forth?
   You shall not stir out of your house today.
CAESAR: Caesar shall forth; the things that threaten'd me,
   Ne'er look'd but on my back: When they shall see
   The face of Caesar, they are vanished.
CALPURNIA: Caesar, I never stood on ceremonies,
   Yet now they fright me: There is one within,
   Besides the things that we have heard and seen,
   Recounts most horrid sights seen by the Watch.
   A lioness hath whelped in the streets,
   And graves have yawn'd, and yielded up their dead;
   Fierce fiery warriors fought upon the clouds
   In ranks and squadrons, and right form of war
   Which drizzl'd blood upon the Capitol:
   The noise of battle hurtled in the air:
   Horses did neigh, and dying men did groan,
   And ghosts did shriek and squeal about the streets.
   O Caesar, these things are beyond all use,
   And I do fear them.
CAESAR: What can be avoided
   Whose end is purpos'd by the mighty Gods?
   Yet Caesar shall go forth: for these predictions
   Are to the world in general, as to Caesar.
CALPURNIA: When beggars die, there are no comets seen,
   The Heavens themselves blaze forth the death of Princes.
CAESAR: Cowards die many times before their deaths,
   The valiant never taste of death but once:
   Of all the wonders that I yet have heard,
   It seems to me most strange that men should fear,
   Seeing that death, a necessary end
   Will come, when it will come.
                    Enter Servant.

What say the Augurers?
SERVANT: They would not have you to stir forth today.
  Plucking the entrails of an offering forth,
  They could not find a heart within the beast.
CAESAR: The Gods do this in shame of cowardice:
  Caesar should be a beast without a heart
  If he should stay at home today for fear:
  No Caesar shall not; Danger knows full well
  That Caesar is more dangerous than he.
  We are two lions litter'd in one day,
  And I the elder and more terrible,
  And Caesar shall go forth.
CALPURNIA: Alas my Lord,
  Your wisdom is consum'd in confidence:
  Do not go forth today: Call it my fear,
  That keeps you in the house, and not your own.
  We'll send Mark Antony to the Senate house,
  And he shall say, you are not well today:
  Let me upon my knee, prevail in this.
CAESAR: Mark Antony shall say I am not well,
  And for thy humour, I will stay at home.
                    Enter Decius.
  Here's Decius Brutus, he shall tell them so.
DECIUS: Caesar, all hail: Good morrow worthy Caesar,
  I come to fetch you to the Senate house.
CAESAR: And you are come in very happy time,
  To bear my greeting to the Senators,
  And tell them that I will not come today:
  Cannot, is false: and that I dare not, falser:
  I will not come today, tell them so Decius.
CALPURNIA: Say he is sick.
CAESAR: Shall Caesar send a lie?
  Have I in conquest stretch'd mine arm so far,

    To be afear'd to tell grey-beards the truth:
    Decius, go tell them, Caesar will not come.
DECIUS: Most mighty Caesar let me know some cause,
    Lest I be laugh'd at when I tell them so.
CAESAR: The cause is in my will, I will not come,
    That is enough to satisfy the Senate.
    But for your private satisfaction,
    Because I love you, I will let you know.
    Calpurnia here my wife, stays me at home:
    She dreamt tonight, she saw my statue,
    Which like a fountain, with an hundred spouts
    Did run pure blood: and many lusty Romans
    Came smiling, and did bathe their hands in it:
    And these does she apply, for warnings and portents,
    And evils imminent; and on her knee
    Hath begg'd, that I will stay at home today.
DECIUS: This dream is all amiss interpreted,
    It was a vision, fair and fortunate:
    Your statue spouting blood in many pipes,
    In which so many smiling Romans bath'd,
    Signifies, that from you great Rome shall suck
    Reviving blood, and that great men shall press
    For tinctures, stains, relics, and cognizance.
    This by Calpurnia's dream is signified.
CAESAR: And this way have you well expounded it.
DECIUS: I have, when you have heard what I can say:
    And know it now, the Senate have concluded
    To give this day, a Crown to mighty Caesar.
    If you shall send them word you will not come,
    Their minds may change. Besides, it were a mock
    Apt to be render'd, for some one to say,
    Break up the Senate, till another time:
    When Caesar's wife shall meet with better dreams.

If Caesar hide himself, shall they not whisper
Lo Caesar is afraid?
Pardon me Caesar, for my dear dear love
To your proceeding, bids me tell you this:
And reason to my love is liable.
CAESAR: How foolish do your fears seem now Calpurnia?
I am ashamed I did yield to them.
Give me my robe, for I will go.
Enter Brutus, Ligarius, Metellus, Casca, Trebonius, Cinna
and Publius.
And look where Publius is come to fetch me.
PUBLIUS: Good morrow Caesar.
CAESAR: Welcome Publius.
What Brutus, are you stirr'd so early too?
Good morrow Casca: Caius Ligarius,
Caesar was ne'er so much your enemy,
As that same ague which hath made you lean.
What is't a'clock?
BRUTUS: Caesar, 'tis strucken eight.
CAESAR: I thank you for your pains and courtesy.
Enter Antony.
See, Antony that revels long a-nights
Is not withstanding up. Good morrow Antony.
ANTONY: So to most noble Caesar.
CAESAR: Bid them prepare within:
I am to blame to be thus waited for.
Now Cinna, now Metellus: what Trebonius,
I have an hour's talk in store for you:
Remember that you call on me today:
Be near me, that I may remember you.
TREBONIUS: Caesar I will: and so near will I be,
That your best friends shall wish I had been further.
CAESAR: Good friends go in, and taste some wine with me.

And we (like friends) will straightway go together.

BRUTUS: That every like is not the same, O Caesar,
The heart of Brutus earns to think upon.

Exeunt.

II. 3

Enter Artemidorus.

ARTEMIDORUS: *Caesar, beware of Brutus, take heed of Cassius; come not near Casca, have an eye to Cinna, trust not Trebonius, mark well Metellus Cimber, Decius Brutus loves thee not: Thou hast wrong'd Caius Ligarius. There is but one mind in all these men, and it is bent against Caesar: If thou beest not immortal, look about you: Security gives way to Conspiracy. The mighty Gods defend thee.*

Thy lover, *Artemidorus.*

Here will I stand, till Caesar pass along,
And as a suitor will I give him this:
My heart laments, that Virtue cannot live
Out of the teeth of Emulation.
If thou read this, O Caesar, thou mayst live;
If not, the Fates with traitors do contrive.

Exit.

II. 4

Enter Portia and Lucius.

PORTIA: I prithee boy, run to the Senate-house,
Stay not to answer me, but get thee gone.
Why dost thou stay?

LUCIUS: To know my errand Madam.

PORTIA: I would have had thee there and here again
Ere I can tell thee what thou shouldst do there:

O Constancy, be strong upon my side,
Set a huge mountain 'tween my heart and tongue:
I have a man's mind, but a woman's might:
How hard it is for women to keep counsel.
Art thou here yet?

LUCIUS: Madam, what should I do?
Run to the Capitol, and nothing else?
And so return to you, and nothing else?

PORTIA: Yes, bring me word boy, if thy Lord look well,
For he went sickly forth: and take good note
What Caesar doth, what suitors press to him.
Hark boy, what noise is that?

LUCIUS: I hear none Madam.

PORTIA: Prithee listen well:
I heard a bustling rumour like a fray,
And the wind brings it from the Capitol.

LUCIUS: Sooth Madam, I hear nothing.

Enter the Soothsayer.

PORTIA: Come hither fellow, which way hast thou been?

SOOTHSAYER: At mine own house, good Lady.

PORTIA: What is't a'clock?

SOOTHSAYER: About the ninth hour Lady.

PORTIA: Is Caesar yet gone to the Capitol?

SOOTHSAYER: Madam not yet, I go to take my stand,
To see him pass on to the Capitol.

PORTIA: Thou hast some suit to Caesar, hast thou not?

SOOTHSAYER: That I have Lady, if it will please Caesar
To be so good to Caesar, as to hear me:
I shall beseech him to befriend himself.

PORTIA: Why know'st thou any harm's intended towards
him?

SOOTHSAYER: None that I know will be,
Much that I fear may chance:

Good morrow to you: here the street is narrow:
The throng that follows Caesar at the heels,
Of Senators, of Praetors, common suitors,
Will crowd a feeble man (almost) to death:
I'll get me to a place more void, and there
Speak to great Caesar as he comes along.

Exit.

PORTIA: I must go in:
Aye me! how weak a thing
The heart of woman is! O Brutus,
The Heavens speed thee in thine enterprise.
Sure the boy heard me: Brutus hath a suit
That Caesar will not grant. O, I grow faint:
Run Lucius, and commend me to my Lord,
Say I am merry; Come to me again,
And bring me word what he doth say to thee.

Exeunt.

III. 1

Flourish.

*Enter Caesar, Brutus, Cassius, Casca, Decius, Metellus,
Trebonius, Cinna, Antony, Lepidus, Artemidorus,
Popilius, Publius, and the Soothsayer.*

CAESAR: The Ides of March are come.

SOOTHSAYER: Ay Caesar, but not gone.

ARTEMIDORUS: Hail Caesar: Read this schedule.

DECIUS: Trebonius doth desire you to o'er-read
(At your best leisure) this his humble suit.

ARTEMIDORUS: O Caesar, read mine first: for mine's a
suit
That touches Caesar nearer. Read it great Caesar.

CAESAR: What touches us ourself, shall be last serv'd.

ARTEMIDORUS: Delay not Caesar, read it instantly.

CAESAR: What, is the fellow mad?

PUBLIUS: Sirrah, give place.

CASSIUS: What, urge you your petitions in the street?
  Come to the Capitol.

POPILIUS: I wish your enterprise today may thrive.

CASSIUS: What enterprise Popilius?

POPILIUS: Fare you well.

BRUTUS: What said Popilius Lena?

CASSIUS: He wish'd today our enterprise might thrive:
  I fear our purpose is discovered.

BRUTUS: Look how he makes to Caesar: mark him.

CASSIUS: Casca be sudden, for we fear prevention.
  Brutus what shall be done? If this be known,
  Cassius or Caesar never shall turn back,
  For I will slay myself.

BRUTUS: Cassius be constant:
  Popilius Lena speaks not of our purposes,
  For look he smiles, and Caesar doth not change.

CASSIUS: Trebonius knows his time: for look you Brutus
  He draws Mark Antony out of the way.

Exeunt Antony and Trebonius.

DECIUS: Where is Metellus Cimber, let him go,
  And presently prefer his suit to Caesar.

BRUTUS: He is address'd: press near, and second him.

CINNA: Casca, you are the first that rears your hand.

CAESAR: Are we all ready? What is now amiss,
  That Caesar and his Senate must redress?

METELLUS: Most high, most mighty, and most puissant
    Caesar,
  Metellus Cimber throws before thy seat
  An humble heart.

CAESAR: I must prevent thee Cimber:

These couchings, and these lowly courtesies
Might fire the blood of ordinary men,
And turn pre-ordinance, and first decree,
Into the law of children. Be not fond,
To think that Caesar bears such rebel blood
That will be thaw'd from the true quality
With that which melteth fools, I mean sweet words,
Low-crooked-court'sies and base spaniel fawning:
Thy Brother by decree is banished:
If thou dost bend, and pray, and fawn for him,
I spurn thee like a cur out of my way:
Know, Caesar doth not wrong, nor without cause
Will he be satisfied.

METELLUS: Is there no voice more worthy than my own,
To sound more sweetly in great Caesar's ear,
For the repealing of my banish'd brother?

BRUTUS: I kiss thy hand, but not in flattery Caesar:
Desiring thee, that Publius Cimber may
Have an immediate freedom of repeal.

CAESAR: What Brutus?

CASSIUS: Pardon Caesar: Caesar pardon:
As low as to thy foot doth Cassius fall,
To beg enfranchisement for Publius Cimber.

CAESAR: I could be well mov'd, if I were as you,
If I could pray to move, prayers would move me:
But I am constant as the Northern Star,
Of whose true fix'd, and resting quality,
There is no fellow in the Firmament.
The skies are painted with unnumber'd sparks,
They are all fire, and every one doth shine:
But, there's but one in all doth hold his place.
So, in the world; 'Tis furnish'd well with men,
And men are flesh and blood, and apprehensive;

Yet in the number, I do know but one
That unassailable holds on his rank,
Unshak'd of motion: and that I am he,
Let me a little show it, even in this:
That I was constant Cimber should be banish'd,
And constant do remain to keep him so.

CINNA: O Caesar.

CAESAR: Hence: Wilt thou lift up Olympus?

DECIUS: Great Caesar.

CAESAR: Doth not Brutus bootless kneel?

CASCA: Speak hands for me.

They stab Caesar.

CAESAR: *Et tu Brute?* – Then fall Caesar.

Dies.

CINNA: Liberty, Freedom; Tyranny is dead,
Run hence, proclaim, cry it about the streets.

CASSIUS: Some to the common pulpits, and cry out
Liberty, Freedom, and Enfranchisement.

BRUTUS: People and Senators, be not affrighted:
Fly not, stand still: Ambition's debt is paid.

CASCA: Go to the pulpit Brutus.

DECIUS: And Cassius too.

BRUTUS: Where's Publius?

CINNA: Here, quite confounded with this mutiny.

METELLUS: Stand fast together, lest some friend of Caesar's
Should chance –

BRUTUS: Talk not of standing. Publius good cheer,
There is no harm intended to your person,
Nor to no Roman else: so tell them Publius.

CASSIUS: And leave us Publius, lest that the people
Rushing on us, should do your age some mischief.

BRUTUS: Do so, and let no man abide this deed,
But we the doers.

Enter Trebonius.

CASCA: Where is Antony?

TREBONIUS: Fled to his house amaz'd:
　Men, wives and children, stare, cry out, and run,
　As it were Doomsday.

BRUTUS: Fates, we will know your pleasures:
　That we shall die we know, 'tis but the time
　And drawing days out, that men stand upon.

CASCA: Why he that cuts off twenty years of life,
　Cuts off so many years of fearing death.

BRUTUS: Grant that, and then is Death a benefit:
　So are we Caesar's friends, that have abridg'd
　His time of fearing death. Stoop Romans, stoop,
　And let us bathe our hands in Caesar's blood
　Up to the elbows, and besmear our swords:
　Then walk we forth, even to the Market-place,
　And waving our red weapons o'er our heads,
　Let's all cry Peace, Freedom, and Liberty.

CASSIUS: Stoop then, and wash. How many ages hence
　Shall this our lofty scene be acted over,
　In states unborn, and accents yet unknown?

BRUTUS: How many times shall Caesar bleed in sport,
　That now on Pompey's basis lies along,
　No worthier than the dust?

CASSIUS: So oft as that shall be,
　So often shall the knot of us be call'd,
　The men that gave their Country liberty.

DECIUS: What, shall we forth?

CASSIUS: Ay, every man away.
　Brutus shall lead, and we will grace his heels
　With the most boldest, and best hearts of Rome.

Enter a Servant.

BRUTUS: Soft, who comes here? A friend of Antony's.

SERVANT: Thus Brutus did my master bid me kneel;
 Thus did Mark Antony bid me fall down,
 And being prostrate, thus he bade me say:
 Brutus is noble, wise, valiant, and honest;
 Caesar was mighty, bold, royal, and loving:
 Say, I love Brutus, and I honour him;
 Say, I fear'd Caesar, honour'd him, and lov'd him.
 If Brutus will vouchsafe, that Antony,
 May safely come to him, and be resolv'd
 How Caesar hath deserv'd to lie in death,
 Mark Antony, shall not love Caesar dead
 So well as Brutus living; but will follow
 The fortunes and affairs of noble Brutus,
 Thorough the hazards of this untrod state,
 With all true faith. So says my master Antony.
BRUTUS: Thy master is a wise and valiant Roman,
 I never thought him worse:
 Tell him, so please him come unto this place
 He shall be satisfied: and by my honour
 Depart untouch'd.
SERVANT: I'll fetch him presently.
                    Exit Servant.
BRUTUS: I know that we shall have him well to friend.
CASSIUS: I wish we may: But yet have I a mind
 That fears him much: and my misgiving still
 Falls shrewdly to the purpose.
                    Enter Antony.
BRUTUS: But here comes Antony:
 Welcome, Mark Antony.
ANTONY: O mighty Caesar! Dost thou lie so low?
 Are all thy conquests, glories, triumphs, spoils,
 Shrunk to this little measure? Fare thee well.
 I know not Gentlemen what you intend,

Who else must be let blood, who else is rank:
If I myself, there is no hour so fit
As Caesar's death's hour; nor no instrument
Of half that worth, as those your swords; made rich
With the most noble blood of all this world.
I do beseech ye, if you bear me hard,
Now, whilst your purpled hands do reek and smoke,
Fulfil your pleasure. Live a thousand years,
I shall not find myself so apt to die.
No place will please me so, no mean of death,
As here by Caesar, and by you cut off,
The choice and master Spirits of this Age.

BRUTUS: O Antony! Beg not your death of us:
Though now we must appear bloody and cruel,
As by our hands, and this our present act
You see we do: Yet see you but our hands,
And this, the bleeding business they have done:
Our hearts you see not, they are pitiful:
And pity to the general wrong of Rome,
As fire drives out fire, so pity, pity
Hath done this deed on Caesar. For your part,
To you, our swords have leaden points Mark Antony:
Our arms in strength of malice, and our hearts
Of Brothers' temper, do receive you in,
With all kind love, good thoughts, and reverence.

CASSIUS: Your voice shall be as strong as any man's,
In the disposing of new dignities.

BRUTUS: Only be patient, till we have appeas'd
The multitude, beside themselves with fear,
And then, we will deliver you the cause,
Why I, that did love Caesar when I struck him,
Have thus proceeded.

ANTONY: I doubt not of your wisdom:

Let each man render me his bloody hand.
First Marcus Brutus will I shake with you;
Next Caius Cassius do I take your hand;
Now Decius Brutus yours; now yours Metellus;
Yours Cinna; and my valiant Casca, yours;
Though last, not least in love, yours good Trebonius:
Gentlemen all: Alas, what shall I say?
My credit now stands on such slippery ground,
That one of two bad ways you must conceit me,
Either a coward, or a flatterer.
That I did love thee Caesar, O 'tis true:
If then thy spirit look upon us now,
Shall it not grieve thee dearer than thy death,
To see thy Antony making his peace,
Shaking the bloody fingers of thy foes?
Most noble, in the presence of thy corse,
Had I as many eyes, as thou hast wounds,
Weeping as fast as they stream forth thy blood,
It would become me better, than to close
In terms of friendship with thine enemies.
Pardon me Julius, here wast thou bay'd brave hart,
Here didst thou fall, and here thy hunters stand
Sign'd in thy spoil, and crimson'd in thy lethe.
O World! thou wast the forest to this hart,
And this indeed, O World, the heart of thee.
How like a deer, strucken by many Princes,
Dost thou here lie?

CASSIUS: Mark Antony.

ANTONY: Pardon me Caius Cassius:
The enemies of Caesar, shall say this:
Then, in a friend, it is cold modesty.

CASSIUS: I blame you not for praising Caesar so,
But what compact mean you to have with us?

Will you be prick'd in number of our friends,
Or shall we on, and not depend on you?

ANTONY: Therefore I took your hands, but was indeed
Sway'd from the point, by looking down on Caesar.
Friends am I with you all, and love you all,
Upon this hope, that you shall give me reasons,
Why, and wherein, Caesar was dangerous.

BRUTUS: Or else were this a savage spectacle:
Our reasons are so full of good regard,
That were you Antony, the son of Caesar,
You should be satisfied.

ANTONY: That's all I seek,
And am moreover suitor, that I may
Produce his body to the Market-place,
And in the Pulpit as becomes a friend,
Speak in the order of his funeral.

BRUTUS: You shall Mark Antony.

CASSIUS: Brutus, a word with you:
You know not what you do; Do not consent
That Antony speak in his funeral:
Know you how much the people may be mov'd
By that which he will utter.

BRUTUS: By your pardon:
I will myself into the Pulpit first,
And show the reason of our Caesar's death.
What Antony shall speak, I will protest
He speaks by leave, and by permission:
And that we are contented Caesar shall
Have all true rites, and lawful ceremonies,
It shall advantage more, than do us wrong.

CASSIUS: I know not what may fall, I like it not.

BRUTUS: Mark Antony, here take you Caesar's body:
You shall not in your funeral speech blame us,

But speak all good you can devise of Caesar,
And say you do't by our permission:
Else shall you not have any hand at all
About his funeral. And you shall speak
In the same Pulpit whereto I am going,
After my speech is ended.

ANTONY: Be it so:
I do desire no more.

BRUTUS: Prepare the body then, and follow us.

Exeunt.

Manet Antony.

ANTONY: O pardon me, thou bleeding piece of earth:
That I am meek and gentle with these butchers.
Thou art the ruins of the noblest man
That ever lived in the tide of times.
Woe to the hand that shed this costly blood.
Over thy wounds, now do I prophesy,
(Which like dumb mouths do ope their ruby lips,
To beg the voice and utterance of my tongue)
A curse shall light upon the limbs of men;
Domestic fury, and fierce civil strife,
Shall cumber all the parts of Italy:
Blood and destruction shall be so in use,
And dreadful objects so familiar,
That mothers shall but smile, when they behold
Their infants quartered with the hands of war:
All pity chok'd with custom of fell deeds,
And Caesar's Spirit ranging for Revenge,
With Ate by his side, come hot from Hell,
Shall in these confines, with a Monarch's voice,
Cry havoc, and let slip the Dogs of War,
That this foul deed, shall smell above the earth
With carrion men, groaning for burial.

Enter Octavius' Servant.

You serve Octavius Caesar, do you not?

SERVANT: I do Mark Antony.

ANTONY: Caesar did write for him to come to Rome.

SERVANT: He did receive his letters, and is coming,
　And bid me say to you by word of mouth –
　O Caesar!

ANTONY: Thy heart is big: get thee apart and weep:
　Passion I see is catching for mine eyes,
　Seeing those beads of sorrow stand in thine,
　Began to water. Is thy Master coming?

SERVANT: He lies tonight within seven leagues of Rome.

ANTONY: Post back with speed,
　And tell him what hath chanc'd:
　Here is a mourning Rome, a dangerous Rome,
　No Rome of safety for Octavius yet,
　Hie hence, and tell him so. Yet stay awhile,
　Thou shalt not back, till I have borne this corse
　Into the Market-place: There shall I try
　In my Oration, how the People take
　The cruel issue of these bloody men,
　According to the which, thou shalt discourse
　To young Octavius, of the state of things.
　Lend me your hand.

Exeunt.

III. 2

*Enter Brutus and goes into the Pulpit, and Cassius,
with the Plebeians.*

PLEBEIANS: We will be satisfied: let us be satisfied.

BRUTUS: Then follow me, and give me audience friends.
　Cassius go you into the other street,

And part the numbers:
Those that will hear me speak, let 'em stay here;
Those that will follow Cassius, go with him,
And public reasons shall be render'd
Of Caesar's death.

1 PLEBEIAN: I will hear Brutus speak.

2 PLEBEIAN: I will hear Cassius, and compare their reasons,
When severally we hear them render'd.

Exit Cassius with some of the Plebeians.

3 PLEBEIAN: The noble Brutus is ascended: Silence.

BRUTUS: Be patient till the last.

Romans, countrymen, and lovers, hear me for my cause,
and be silent, that you may hear. Believe me for mine
honour, and have respect to mine honour, that you may
believe. Censure me in your wisdom, and awake your
sense, that you may the better judge. If there be any in
this Assembly, any dear friend of Caesar's, to him I say,
that Brutus' love to Caesar, was no less than his. If then,
that friend demand, why Brutus rose against Caesar, this
is my answer: Not that I lov'd Caesar less, but that I
lov'd Rome more. Had you rather Caesar were living,
and die all slaves; than that Caesar were dead, to live all
free men? As Caesar lov'd me, I weep for him; as he was
fortunate, I rejoice at it; as he was valiant, I honour him:
But, as he was ambitious, I slew him. There is tears, for
his love: joy, for his fortune: honour, for his valour: and
death, for his ambition. Who is here so base, that would
be a bondman? If any, speak, for him have I offended.
Who is here so rude, that would not be a Roman? If any,
speak, for him have I offended. Who is here so vile, that
will not love his Country? If any, speak, for him have I
offended. I pause for a reply.

ALL: None Brutus, none.

BRUTUS: Then none have I offended. I have done no more
to Caesar, than you shall do to Brutus. The question of
his death, is enroll'd in the Capitol: his glory not extenuated, wherein he was worthy; nor his offences enforc'd,
for which he suffered death.

Enter Mark Antony, with Caesar's body.

Here comes his body, mourn'd by Mark Antony, who
though he had no hand in his death, shall receive the
benefit of his dying, a place in the Commonwealth, as
which of you shall not. With this I depart, that as I slew
my best lover for the good of Rome, I have the same
dagger for myself, when it shall please my country to
need my death.

ALL: Live Brutus, live, live.

1 PLEBEIAN: Bring him with triumph home unto his
house.

2 PLEBEIAN: Give him a statue with his ancestors.

3 PLEBEIAN: Let him be Caesar.

4 PLEBEIAN: Caesar's better parts,
Shall be crown'd in Brutus.

1 PLEBEIAN: We'll bring him to his house,
With shouts and clamours.

BRUTUS: My countrymen.

2 PLEBEIAN: Peace, silence, Brutus speaks.

1 PLEBEIAN: Peace ho.

BRUTUS: Good countrymen, let me depart alone,
And (for my sake) stay here with Antony:
Do grace to Caesar's corpse, and grace his speech
Tending to Caesar's glories, which Mark Antony
(By our permission) is allow'd to make.
I do entreat you, not a man depart
Save I alone, till Antony have spoke.

Exit.

1 PLEBEIAN: Stay ho, and let us hear Mark Antony.

3 PLEBEIAN: Let him go up into the public Chair,
We'll hear him: Noble Antony go up.

ANTONY: For Brutus' sake, I am beholding to you.

4 PLEBEIAN: What does he say of Brutus?

3 PLEBEIAN: He says, for Brutus' sake
He finds himself beholding to us all.

4 PLEBEIAN: 'Twere best he speak no harm of Brutus
here!

1 PLEBEIAN: This Caesar was a tyrant.

3 PLEBEIAN: Nay that's certain:
We are blest that Rome is rid of him.

2 PLEBEIAN: Peace, let us hear what Antony can say.

ANTONY: You gentle Romans.

ALL: Peace ho, let us hear him.

ANTONY: Friends, Romans, countrymen, lend me your
ears:
I come to bury Caesar, not to praise him:
The evil that men do, lives after them,
The good is oft interred with their bones,
So let it be with Caesar. The noble Brutus,
Hath told you Caesar was ambitious:
If it were so, it was a grievous fault,
And grievously hath Caesar answer'd it.
Here, under leave of Brutus, and the rest
(For Brutus is an honourable man,
So are they all; all honourable men)
Come I to speak in Caesar's funeral.
He was my friend, faithful, and just to me;
But Brutus says, he was ambitious,
And Brutus is an honourable man.
He hath brought many captives home to Rome,
Whose ransoms, did the general coffers fill:

Did this in Caesar seem ambitious?
When that the poor have cried, Caesar hath wept:
Ambition should be made of sterner stuff,
Yet Brutus says, he was ambitious:
And Brutus is an honourable man.
You all did see, that on the Lupercal,
I thrice presented him a kingly Crown,
Which he did thrice refuse. Was this ambition?
Yet Brutus says, he was ambitious:
And sure he is an honourable man.
I speak not to disprove what Brutus spoke,
But here I am, to speak what I do know;
You all did love him once, not without cause,
What cause withholds you then, to mourn for him?
O Judgement! thou art fled to brutish beasts,
And men have lost their reason. Bear with me,
My heart is in the coffin there with Caesar,
And I must pause, till it come back to me.

1 PLEBEIAN: Methinks there is much reason in his sayings.

2 PLEBEIAN: If thou consider rightly of the matter,
Caesar has had great wrong.

3 PLEBEIAN: Has he masters? I fear there will a worse come
in his place.

4 PLEBEIAN: Mark'd ye his words? He would not take the
Crown,
Therefore 'tis certain, he was not ambitious.

1 PLEBEIAN: If it be found so, some will dear abide it.

2 PLEBEIAN: Poor soul, his eyes are red as fire with weeping.

3 PLEBEIAN: There's not a nobler man in Rome than
Antony.

4 PLEBEIAN: Now mark him, he begins again to speak.

ANTONY: But yesterday, the word of Caesar might

Have stood against the World: Now lies he there,
And none so poor to do him reverence.
O Masters! if I were dispos'd to stir
Your hearts and minds to mutiny and rage,
I should do Brutus wrong, and Cassius wrong:
Who (you all know) are honourable men.
I will not do them wrong: I rather choose
To wrong the dead, to wrong myself and you,
Than I will wrong such honourable men.
But here's a parchment, with the seal of Caesar,
I found it in his closet, 'tis his Will:
Let but the Commons hear this testament:
(Which pardon me) I do not mean to read,
And they would go and kiss dead Caesar's wounds,
And dip their napkins in his sacred blood;
Yea, beg a hair of him for memory,
And dying, mention it within their Wills,
Bequeathing it as a rich legacy
Unto their issue.

4 PLEBEIAN: We'll hear the Will, read it Mark Antony.
ALL: The Will, the Will; we will hear Caesar's Will.
ANTONY: Have patience gentle friends, I must not read it.
It is not meet you know how Caesar lov'd you:
You are not wood, you are not stones, but men:
And being men, hearing the Will of Caesar,
It will inflame you, it will make you mad:
'Tis good you know not that you are his heirs,
For if you should, O what would come of it?
4 PLEBEIAN: Read the Will, we'll hear it Antony:
You shall read us the Will, Caesar's Will.
ANTONY: Will you be patient? Will you stay awhile?
I have o'ershot myself to tell you of it,
I fear I wrong the honourable men,

Whose daggers have stabb'd Caesar: I do fear it.

4 PLEBEIAN: They were traitors: honourable men?

ALL: The Will, the Testament.

2 PLEBEIAN: They were villains, murderers: the Will, read the Will.

ANTONY: You will compel me then to read the Will:
Then make a ring about the corpse of Caesar,
And let me show you him that made the Will:
Shall I descend? And will you give me leave?

ALL: Come down.

2 PLEBEIAN: Descend.

3 PLEBEIAN: You shall have leave.

4 PLEBEIAN: A ring, stand round.

I PLEBEIAN: Stand from the hearse, stand from the body.

2 PLEBEIAN: Room for Antony, most noble Antony.

ANTONY: Nay press not so upon me, stand far off.

ALL: Stand back: room, bear back.

ANTONY: If you have tears, prepare to shed them now.
You all do know this mantle, I remember
The first time ever Caesar put it on,
'Twas on a summer's evening in his tent,
That day he overcame the Nervii.
Look, in this place ran Cassius' dagger through:
See what a rent the envious Casca made:
Through this, the well-beloved Brutus stabb'd,
And as he pluck'd his cursed steel away:
Mark how the blood of Caesar follow'd it,
As rushing out of doors, to be resolv'd
If Brutus so unkindly knock'd, or no:
For Brutus, as you know, was Caesar's Angel.
Judge, O you Gods, how dearly Caesar lov'd him:
This was the most unkindest cut of all.
For when the noble Caesar saw him stab,

Ingratitude, more strong than traitors' arms,
Quite vanquish'd him: then burst his mighty heart,
And in his mantle, muffling up his face,
Even at the base of Pompey's statue
(Which all the while ran blood) great Caesar fell.
O what a fall was there, my countrymen?
Then I, and you, and all of us fell down,
Whilst bloody Treason flourish'd over us.
O now you weep, and I perceive you feel
The dint of pity: These are gracious drops.
Kind souls, what weep you, when you but behold
Our Caesar's vesture wounded? Look you here,
Here is himself, marr'd as you see, with traitors.

1 PLEBEIAN: O piteous spectacle!

2 PLEBEIAN: O noble Caesar!

3 PLEBEIAN: O woeful day!

4 PLEBEIAN: O traitors, villains!

1 PLEBEIAN: O most bloody sight!

2 PLEBEIAN: We will be reveng'd: Revenge,
About, seek, burn, fire, kill, slay,
Let not a traitor live.

ANTONY: Stay countrymen.

1 PLEBEIAN: Peace there, hear the noble Antony.

2 PLEBEIAN: We'll hear him, we'll follow him, we'll die
with him.

ANTONY: Good friends, sweet friends, let me not stir you
up
To such a sudden flood of mutiny:
They that have done this deed, are honourable.
What private griefs they have, alas I know not,
That made them do it: they are wise, and honourable,
And will no doubt with reasons answer you.
I come not (friends) to steal away your hearts,

I am no orator, as Brutus is;
But (as you know me all) a plain blunt man
That love my friend, and that they know full well,
That gave me public leave to speak of him:
For I have neither writ nor words, nor worth,
Action, nor utterance, nor the power of speech,
To stir men's blood. I only speak right on:
I tell you that, which you yourselves do know,
Show you sweet Caesar's wounds, poor poor dumb
    mouths
And bid them speak for me: but were I Brutus,
And Brutus Antony, there were an Antony
Would ruffle up your spirits, and put a tongue
In every wound of Caesar, that should move
The stones of Rome, to rise and mutiny.

ALL: We'll mutiny.

1 PLEBEIAN: We'll burn the house of Brutus.

3 PLEBEIAN: Away then, come, seek the conspirators.

ANTONY: Yet hear me countrymen, yet hear me speak.

ALL: Peace ho, hear Antony, most noble Antony.

ANTONY: Why friends, you go to do you know not what:
    Wherein hath Caesar thus deserv'd your loves?
    Alas you know not, I must tell you then:
    You have forgot the Will I told you of.

ALL: Most true, the Will, let's stay and hear the Will.

ANTONY: Here is the Will, and under Caesar's seal:
    To every Roman citizen he gives,
    To every several man, seventy five drachmas.

2 PLEBEIAN: Most noble Caesar, we'll revenge his death.

3 PLEBEIAN: O royal Caesar.

ANTONY: Hear me with patience.

ALL: Peace ho.

ANTONY: Moreover, he hath left you all his walks,

His private arbours, and new-planted orchards,
On this side Tiber, he hath left them you,
And to your heirs for ever: common pleasures
To walk abroad, and recreate yourselves.
Here was a Caesar: when comes such another?
1 PLEBEIAN: Never, never: come, away, away:
We'll burn his body in the holy place,
And with the brands fire the traitors' houses.
Take up the body.
2 PLEBEIAN: Go fetch fire.
3 PLEBEIAN: Pluck down benches.
4 PLEBEIAN: Pluck down forms, windows, anything.
                    Exeunt Plebeians with the body.
ANTONY: Now let it work: Mischief thou art afoot,
Take thou what course thou wilt.
How now fellow?
                    Enter a Servant.
SERVANT: Sir, Octavius is already come to Rome.
ANTONY: Where is he?
SERVANT: He and Lepidus are at Caesar's house.
ANTONY: And thither will I straight, to visit him:
He comes upon a wish. Fortune is merry,
And in this mood will give us any thing.
SERVANT: I heard him say, Brutus and Cassius
Are rid like madmen through the gates of Rome.
ANTONY: Belike they had some notice of the people
How I had mov'd them. Bring me to Octavius.
                    Exeunt.

III. 3

Enter Cinna the Poet, and after him the Plebeians.

CINNA: I dreamt tonight, that I did feast with Caesar,
And things unluckily charge my fantasy:
I have no will to wander forth of doors,
Yet something leads me forth.

1 PLEBEIAN: What is your name?

2 PLEBEIAN: Whither are you going?

3 PLEBEIAN: Where do you dwell?

4 PLEBEIAN: Are you a married man, or a bachelor?

2 PLEBEIAN: Answer every man directly.

1 PLEBEIAN: Ay, and briefly.

4 PLEBEIAN: Ay, and wisely.

3 PLEBEIAN: Ay, and truly, you were best.

CINNA: What is my name? Whither am I going? Where
do I dwell? Am I a married man, or a bachelor? Then to
answer every man, directly and briefly, wisely and truly:
wisely I say, I am a bachelor.

2 PLEBEIAN: That's as much as to say, they are fools that
marry: you'll bear me a bang for that I fear: proceed
directly.

CINNA: Directly I am going to Caesar's funeral.

1 PLEBEIAN: As a friend, or an enemy?

CINNA: As a friend.

2 PLEBEIAN: That matter is answered directly.

4 PLEBEIAN: For your dwelling: briefly.

CINNA: Briefly, I dwell by the Capitol.

3 PLEBEIAN: Your name sir, truly.

CINNA: Truly, my name is Cinna.

1 PLEBEIAN: Tear him to pieces, he's a conspirator.

CINNA: I am Cinna the Poet, I am Cinna the Poet.

4 PLEBEIAN: Tear him for his bad verses, tear him for his
bad verses.

CINNA: I am not Cinna the conspirator.

4 PLEBEIAN: It is no matter, his name's Cinna, pluck but
his name out of his heart, and turn him going.

3 PLEBEIAN: Tear him, tear him; Come brands ho, firebrands: to Brutus', to Cassius', burn all. Some to Decius'
house, and some to Casca's; some to Ligarius': Away,
go.

Exeunt all the Plebeians.

IV.1

Enter Antony, Octavius, and Lepidus.

ANTONY: These many then shall die, their names are
prick'd.

OCTAVIUS: Your brother too must die: consent you Lepidus?

LEPIDUS: I do consent.

OCTAVIUS: Prick him down Antony.

LEPIDUS: Upon condition Publius shall not live,
Who is your sister's son, Mark Antony.

ANTONY: He shall not live; look, with a spot I damn him.
But Lepidus, go you to Caesar's house:
Fetch the Will hither, and we shall determine
How to cut off some charge in legacies.

LEPIDUS: What? shall I find you here?

OCTAVIUS: Or here, or at the Capitol.

Exit Lepidus.

ANTONY: This is a slight unmeritable man,
Meet to be sent on errands: is it fit
The three-fold World divided, he should stand
One of the three to share it?

OCTAVIUS: So you thought him,
   And took his voice who should be prick'd to die
   In our black sentence and proscription.
ANTONY: Octavius, I have seen more days than you,
   And though we lay these honours on this man,
   To ease ourselves of divers sland'rous loads,
   He shall but bear them, as the ass bears gold,
   To groan and sweat under the business,
   Either led or driven, as we point the way:
   And having brought our treasure, where we will,
   Then take we down his load, and turn him off
   (Like to the empty ass) to shake his ears,
   And graze in commons.
OCTAVIUS: You may do your will:
   But he's a tried, and valiant soldier.
ANTONY: So is my horse Octavius, and for that
   I do appoint him store of provender.
   It is a creature that I teach to fight,
   To wind, to stop, to run directly on:
   His corporal motion, govern'd by my spirit,
   And in some taste, is Lepidus but so:
   He must be taught, and train'd, and bid go forth:
   A barren-spirited fellow; one that feeds
   On abjects, orts, and imitations,
   Which out of use, and stal'd by other men
   Begin his fashion. Do not talk of him,
   But as a property: and now Octavius,
   Listen great things. Brutus and Cassius
   Are levying powers; we must straight make head:
   Therefore let our alliance be combin'd,
   Our best friends made, our means stretch'd,
   And let us presently go sit in Council,
   How covert matters may be best disclos'd,

And open perils surest answered.

OCTAVIUS: Let us do so: for we are at the stake,
  And bay'd about with many enemies,
  And some that smile have in their hearts I fear
  Millions of mischiefs.

Exeunt.

IV.2

*Drum. Enter Brutus, Lucilius and the Army. Titinius
and Pindarus meet them.*

BRUTUS: Stand ho.

LUCILIUS: Give the word ho, and stand.

BRUTUS: What now Lucilius, is Cassius near?

LUCILIUS: He is at hand, and Pindarus is come
  To do you salutation from his Master.

BRUTUS: He greets me well. Your Master Pindarus
  In his own change, or by ill officers,
  Hath given me some worthy cause to wish
  Things done, undone: But if he be at hand
  I shall be satisfied.

PINDARUS: I do not doubt
  But that my noble Master will appear
  Such as he is, full of regard, and honour.

BRUTUS: He is not doubted. A word Lucilius
  How he receiv'd you: let me be resolv'd.

LUCILIUS: With courtesy, and with respect enough,
  But not with such familiar instances,
  Nor with such free and friendly conference
  As he hath us'd of old.

BRUTUS: Thou hast describ'd
  A hot friend, cooling: Ever note Lucilius,
  When Love begins to sicken and decay

It useth an enforced ceremony.
There are no tricks, in plain and simple Faith:
But hollow men, like horses hot at hand,
Make gallant show, and promise of their mettle:

Low march within.

But when they should endure the bloody spur,
They fall their crests, and like deceitful jades
Sink in the trial. Comes his Army on?

LUCILIUS: They mean this night in Sardis to be quarter'd:
The greater part, the horse in general
Are come with Cassius.

Enter Cassius and his Powers.

BRUTUS: Hark, he is arriv'd:
March gently on to meet him.

CASSIUS: Stand ho.

BRUTUS: Stand ho, speak the word along.

1 SOLDIER: Stand.

2 SOLDIER: Stand.

3 SOLDIER: Stand.

CASSIUS: Most noble Brother, you have done me wrong.

BRUTUS: Judge me you Gods; wrong I mine enemies?
And if not so, how should I wrong a Brother?

CASSIUS: Brutus, this sober form of yours, hides wrongs,
And when you do them –

BRUTUS: Cassius, be content,
Speak your griefs softly, I do know you well.
Before the eyes of both our Armies here
(Which should perceive nothing but love from us)
Let us not wrangle. Bid them move away:
Then in my tent Cassius enlarge your griefs,
And I will give you audience.

CASSIUS: Pindarus,
Bid our Commanders lead their charges off

A little from this ground.

BRUTUS: Lucilius, do you the like, and let no man
Come to our tent, till we have done our conference.
Let Lucius and Titinius guard our door.

Exeunt. Manent Brutus and Cassius.

CASSIUS: That you have wrong'd me, doth appear in this:
You have condemn'd, and noted Lucius Pella
For taking bribes here of the Sardians;
Wherein my letters, praying on his side,
Because I knew the man was slighted off.

BRUTUS: You wrong'd yourself to write in such a case.

CASSIUS: In such a time as this, it is not meet
That every nice offence should bear his comment.

BRUTUS: Let me tell you Cassius, you yourself
Are much condemn'd to have an itching palm,
To sell, and mart your offices for gold
To undeservers.

CASSIUS: I, an itching palm?
You know that you are Brutus that speaks this,
Or by the Gods, this speech were else your last.

BRUTUS: The name of Cassius honours this corruption,
And chastisement doth therefore hide his head.

CASSIUS: Chastisement?

BRUTUS: Remember March, the Ides of March remember:
Did not great Julius bleed for Justice' sake?
What villain touch'd his body, that did stab,
And not for Justice? What? Shall one of us,
That struck the foremost man of all this World,
But for supporting robbers: shall we now,
Contaminate our fingers, with base bribes?
And sell the mighty space of our large honours
For so much trash, as may be grasped thus?
I had rather be a dog, and bay the Moon,

Than such a Roman.

CASSIUS: Brutus, bait not me,
I'll not endure it: you forget yourself
To hedge me in. I am a soldier, I,
Older in practice, abler than yourself
To make conditions.

BRUTUS: Go to: you are not Cassius.

CASSIUS: I am.

BRUTUS: I say, you are not.

CASSIUS: Urge me no more, I shall forget myself:
Have mind upon your health: Tempt me no farther.

BRUTUS: Away slight man.

CASSIUS: Is't possible?

BRUTUS: Hear me, for I will speak.
Must I give way, and room to your rash choler?
Shall I be frighted, when a madman stares?

CASSIUS: O ye Gods, ye Gods, must I endure all this?

BRUTUS: All this? Ay more: fret till your proud heart
break.
Go show your slaves how choleric you are,
And make your bondmen tremble. Must I budge?
Must I observe you? Must I stand and crouch
Under your testy humour? By the Gods,
You shall digest the venom of your spleen
Though it do split you. For, from this day forth,
I'll use you for my mirth, yea for my laughter
When you are waspish.

CASSIUS: Is it come to this?

BRUTUS: You say, you are a better soldier:
Let it appear so; make your vaunting true,
And it shall please me well. For mine own part,
I shall be glad to learn of noble men.

CASSIUS: You wrong me every way:

You wrong me Brutus:
I said, an elder soldier, not a better.
Did I say better?
BRUTUS: If you did, I care not.
CASSIUS: When Caesar liv'd, he durst not thus have mov'd
      me.
BRUTUS: Peace, peace, you durst not so have tempted him.
CASSIUS: I durst not?
BRUTUS: No.
CASSIUS: What? durst not tempt him?
BRUTUS: For your life you durst not.
CASSIUS: Do not presume too much upon my love,
      I may do that I shall be sorry for.
BRUTUS: You have done that you should be sorry for.
      There is no terror Cassius in your threats:
      For I am arm'd so strong in honesty,
      That they pass by me, as the idle wind,
      Which I respect not. I did send to you
      For certain sums of gold, which you deni'd me,
      For I can raise no money by vile means:
      By Heaven, I had rather coin my heart,
      And drop my blood for drachmas, than to wring
      From the hard hands of peasants, their vile trash
      By any indirection. I did send
      To you for gold to pay my Legions,
      Which you deni'd me: was that done like Cassius?
      Should I have answer'd Caius Cassius so?
      When Marcus Brutus grows so covetous,
      To lock such rascal counters from his friends,
      Be ready Gods with all your thunder-bolts,
      Dash him to pieces.
CASSIUS: I deni'd you not.
BRUTUS: You did.

CASSIUS: I did not. He was but a fool
   That brought my answer back. Brutus hath riv'd my
      heart:
   A friend should bear his friend's infirmities;
   But Brutus makes mine greater than they are.
BRUTUS: I do not, till you practise them on me.
CASSIUS: You love me not.
BRUTUS: I do not like your faults.
CASSIUS: A friendly eye could never see such faults.
BRUTUS: A flatterer's would not, though they do appear
   As huge as high Olympus.
CASSIUS: Come Antony, and young Octavius come,
   Revenge yourselves alone on Cassius,
   For Cassius is a-weary of the World:
   Hated by one he loves, brav'd by his Brother,
   Check'd like a bondman, all his faults observ'd,
   Set in a note-book, learn'd, and conn'd by rote
   To cast into my teeth. O I could weep
   My spirit from mine eyes. There is my dagger,
   And here my naked breast: within, a heart
   Dearer than Pluto's mine, richer than gold:
   If that thou be'st a Roman, take it forth.
   I that deni'd thee gold, will give my heart:
   Strike as thou didst at Caesar: For I know,
   When thou didst hate him worst, thou lovedst him better
   Than ever thou lovedst Cassius.
BRUTUS: Sheathe your dagger:
   Be angry when you will, it shall have scope:
   Do what you will, dishonour, shall be humour.
   O Cassius, you are yoked with a lamb
   That carries anger, as the flint bears fire,
   Who much enforced, shows a hasty spark,
   And straight is cold again.

CASSIUS: Hath Cassius liv'd
   To be but mirth and laughter to his Brutus,
   When grief and blood ill temper'd, vexeth him?
BRUTUS: When I spoke that, I was ill temper'd too.
CASSIUS: Do you confess so much? Give me your hand.
BRUTUS: And my heart too.
CASSIUS: O Brutus!
BRUTUS: What's the matter?
CASSIUS: Have not you love enough to bear with me,
   When that rash humour which my Mother gave me
   Makes me forgetful?
BRUTUS: Yes Cassius, and from henceforth
   When you are over-earnest with your Brutus,
   He'll think your Mother chides, and leave you so.
                    Enter a Poet.
POET: Let me go in to see the Generals,
   There is some grudge between 'em, 'tis not meet
   They be alone.
LUCILIUS: You shall not come to them.
POET: Nothing but death shall stay me.
CASSIUS: How now? What's the matter?
POET: For shame you Generals; what do you mean?
   Love, and be friends, as two such men should be,
   For I have seen more years I'm sure than ye.
CASSIUS: Ha, ha, how vilely doth this Cynic rhyme?
BRUTUS: Get you hence sirrah: saucy fellow, hence.
CASSIUS: Bear with him Brutus, 'tis his fashion.
BRUTUS: I'll know his humour, when he knows his time:
   What should the wars do with these jigging fools?
   Companion, hence.
CASSIUS: Away, away be gone.
                    Exit Poet.
BRUTUS: Lucilius and Titinius bid the commanders

Prepare to lodge their companies tonight.

CASSIUS: And come yourselves, and bring Messala with
  you
  Immediately to us.
> *Exeunt Lucilius and Titinius.*

BRUTUS: Lucius, a bowl of wine.
> *Exit Lucius.*

CASSIUS: I did not think you could have been so angry.

BRUTUS: O Cassius, I am sick of many griefs.

CASSIUS: Of your Philosophy you make no use,
  If you give place to accidental evils.

BRUTUS: No man bears sorrow better. Portia is dead.

CASSIUS: Ha? Portia?

BRUTUS: She is dead.

CASSIUS: How 'scap'd I killing, when I cross'd you so?
  O insupportable, and touching loss!
  Upon what sickness?

BRUTUS: Impatient of my absence,
  And grief, that young Octavius with Mark Antony
  Have made themselves so strong: For with her death
  That tidings came. With this she fell distract
  And (her attendants absent) swallow'd fire.

CASSIUS: And died so?

BRUTUS: Even so.

CASSIUS: O ye immortal Gods!
> *Enter Boy with wine, and tapers.*

BRUTUS: Speak no more of her: Give me a bowl of wine,
  In this I bury all unkindness Cassius.   *Drinks.*

CASSIUS: My heart is thirsty for that noble pledge.
  Fill Lucius, till the wine o'er-swell the cup:
  I cannot drink too much of Brutus' love.
> *Exit Lucius.*
> *Enter Titinius and Messala.*

BRUTUS: Come in, Titinius:
  Welcome good Messala:
  Now sit we close about this taper here,
  And call in question our necessities.

CASSIUS: Portia, art thou gone?

BRUTUS: No more I pray you.
  Messala, I have here receiv'd letters,
  That young Octavius, and Mark Antony
  Come down upon us with a mighty power,
  Bending their expedition toward Philippi.

MESSALA: Myself have letters of the self-same tenour.

BRUTUS: With what addition?

MESSALA: That by proscription, and bills of outlawry,
  Octavius, Antony, and Lepidus,
  Have put to death an hundred Senators.

BRUTUS: Therein our letters do not well agree:
  Mine speak of seventy Senators, that died
  By their proscription, Cicero being one.

CASSIUS: Cicero one?

MESSALA: Cicero is dead, and by that order of proscription.
  Had you your letters from your wife, my Lord?

BRUTUS: No Messala.

MESSALA: Nor nothing in your letters writ of her?

BRUTUS: Nothing Messala.

MESSALA: That methinks is strange.

BRUTUS: Why ask you?
  Hear you aught of her, in yours?

MESSALA: No my Lord.

BRUTUS: Now as you are a Roman tell me true.

MESSALA: Then like a Roman, bear the truth I tell,
  For certain she is dead, and by strange manner.

BRUTUS: Why farewell Portia: We must die Messala:
  With meditating that she must die once,

I have the patience to endure it now.

MESSALA: Even so great men, great losses should endure.

CASSIUS: I have as much of this in Art as you,
But yet my Nature could not bear it so.

BRUTUS: Well, to our work alive. What do you think
Of marching to Philippi presently?

CASSIUS: I do not think it good.

BRUTUS: Your reason?

CASSIUS: This it is:
'Tis better that the enemy seek us,
So shall he waste his means, weary his soldiers,
Doing himself offence, whilst we lying still,
Are full of rest, defence, and nimbleness.

BRUTUS: Good reasons must of force give place to better:
The people 'twixt Philippi, and this ground
Do stand but in a forc'd affection:
For they have grudg'd us contribution.
The enemy, marching along by them,
By them shall make a fuller number up,
Come on refresh'd, new added, and encourag'd;
From which advantage shall we cut him off,
If at Philippi we do face him there,
These people at our back.

CASSIUS: Hear me good Brother.

BRUTUS: Under your pardon. You must note beside,
That we have tried the utmost of our friends:
Our legions are brim full, our cause is ripe,
The enemy increaseth every day,
We at the height, are ready to decline.
There is a tide in the affairs of men,
Which taken at the flood, leads on to fortune:
Omitted, all the voyage of their life,
Is bound in shallows, and in miseries.

On such a full sea are we now afloat,
And we must take the current when it serves,
Or lose our ventures.

CASSIUS: Then with your will go on: we'll along
Ourselves, and meet them at Philippi.

BRUTUS: The deep of night is crept upon our talk,
And Nature must obey Necessity,
Which we will niggard with a little rest:
There is no more to say.

CASSIUS: No more, good night:
Early tomorrow will we rise, and hence.

Enter Lucius.

BRUTUS: Lucius my gown: farewell good Messala,

Exit Lucius.

Good night Titinius: Noble, noble Cassius,
Good night, and good repose.

CASSIUS: O my dear Brother:
This was an ill beginning of the night:
Never come such division 'tween our souls:
Let it not Brutus.

Enter Lucius with the gown.

BRUTUS: Every thing is well.

CASSIUS: Good night my Lord.

BRUTUS: Good night good Brother.

TITINIUS: MESSALA: Good night Lord Brutus.

BRUTUS: Farewell every one.

Exeunt Cassius, Titinius and Messala.

Give me the gown. Where is thy instrument?

LUCIUS: Here in the tent.

BRUTUS: What, thou speak'st drowsily?
Poor knave I blame thee not, thou art o'er-watch'd.
Call Claudius, and some other of my men,
I'll have them sleep on cushions in my tent.

LUCIUS: Varro and Claudius.
                    Enter Varro and Claudius.
VARRO: Calls my Lord?
BRUTUS: I pray you sirs, lie in my tent and sleep,
    It may be I shall raise you by and by
    On business to my brother Cassius.
VARRO: So please you, we will stand,
    And watch your pleasure.
BRUTUS: I will not have it so: Lie down good sirs,
    It may be I shall otherwise bethink me.
    Look Lucius, here's the book I sought for so:
    I put it in the pocket of my gown.
LUCIUS: I was sure your Lordship did not give it me.
BRUTUS: Bear with me good Boy, I am much forgetful.
    Canst thou hold up thy heavy eyes awhile,
    And touch thy instrument a strain or two?
LUCIUS: Ay my Lord, an't please you.
BRUTUS: It does my Boy:
    I trouble thee too much, but thou art willing.
LUCIUS: It is my duty Sir.
BRUTUS: I should not urge thy duty past thy might,
    I know young bloods look for a time of rest.
LUCIUS: I have slept my Lord already.
BRUTUS: It was well done, and thou shalt sleep again:
    I will not hold thee long. If I do live,
    I will be good to thee.
                    Music, and a song.
    This is a sleepy tune. O murd'rous slumber!
    Lay'st thou thy leaden mace upon my Boy,
    That plays thee music? Gentle knave good night:
    I will not do thee so much wrong to wake thee:
    If thou dost nod, thou break'st thy instrument,
    I'll take it from thee, and (good Boy) good night.

Let me see, let me see; is not the leaf turn'd down
Where I left reading? Here it is I think.
                    Enter the Ghost of Caesar.
How ill this taper burns. Ha! Who comes here?
I think it is the weakness of mine eyes
That shapes this monstrous Apparition.
It comes upon me: Art thou any thing?
Art thou some God, some Angel, or some Devil,
That makest my blood cold, and my hair to stare?
Speak to me, what thou art?

GHOST: Thy evil Spirit Brutus!

BRUTUS: Why com'st thou?

GHOST: To tell thee thou shalt see me at Philippi.

BRUTUS: Well: then I shall see thee again?

GHOST: Ay, at Philippi.

BRUTUS: Why I will see thee at Philippi then:
                    Exit Ghost.
Now I have taken heart, thou vanishest.
Ill Spirit, I would hold more talk with thee.
Boy, Lucius, Varro, Claudius, sirs: Awake,
Claudius.

LUCIUS: The strings my Lord, are false.

BRUTUS: He thinks he still is at his instrument.
Lucius, awake.

LUCIUS: My Lord.

BRUTUS: Didst thou dream Lucius, that thou so criedst
out?

LUCIUS: My Lord, I do not know that I did cry.

BRUTUS: Yes that thou didst: Didst thou see any thing?

LUCIUS: Nothing my Lord.

BRUTUS: Sleep again Lucius: Sirrah Claudius, fellow,
Thou: Awake.

VARRO: My Lord.

CLAUDIUS: My Lord.

BRUTUS: Why did you so cry out sirs, in your sleep?

BOTH: Did we my Lord?

BRUTUS: Ay: saw you any thing?

VARRO: No my Lord, I saw nothing.

CLAUDIUS: Nor I my Lord.

BRUTUS: Go, and commend me to my Brother Cassius:
　　Bid him set on his powers betimes before,
　　And we will follow.

BOTH: It shall be done my Lord.

Exeunt.

V. 1

Enter Octavius, Antony, and their Army.

OCTAVIUS: Now Antony, our hopes are answered,
　　You said the enemy would not come down,
　　But keep the hills and upper regions:
　　It proves not so: their battles are at hand,
　　They mean to warn us at Philippi here:
　　Answering before we do demand of them.

ANTONY: Tut I am in their bosoms, and I know
　　Wherefore they do it: They could be content
　　To visit other places, and come down
　　With fearful bravery: thinking by this face
　　To fasten in our thoughts that they have courage;
　　But 'tis not so.

Enter a Messenger.

MESSENGER: Prepare you Generals,
　　The enemy comes on in gallant show:
　　Their bloody sign of battle is hung out,
　　And something to be done immediately.

ANTONY: Octavius, lead your battle softly on

Upon the left hand of the even field.

OCTAVIUS: Upon the right hand I, keep thou the left.

ANTONY: Why do you cross me in this exigent?

OCTAVIUS: I do not cross you: but I will do so.

March.

Drum. Enter Brutus, Cassius, and their Army.

BRUTUS: They stand, and would have parley.

CASSIUS: Stand fast Titinius, we must out and talk.

OCTAVIUS: Mark Antony, shall we give sign of battle?

ANTONY: No Caesar, we will answer on their charge.
   Make forth, the Generals would have some words.

OCTAVIUS: Stir not until the signal.

BRUTUS: Words before blows: is it so countrymen?

OCTAVIUS: Not that we love words better, as you do.

BRUTUS: Good words are better than bad strokes, Octavius.

ANTONY: In your bad strokes Brutus, you give good
   words;
   Witness the hole you made in Caesar's heart,
   Crying Long live, hail Caesar.

CASSIUS: Antony,
   The posture of your blows are yet unknown;
   But for your words, they rob the Hybla bees,
   And leave them honeyless.

ANTONY: Not stingless too.

BRUTUS: O yes, and soundless too:
   For you have stol'n their buzzing Antony,
   And very wisely threat before you sting.

ANTONY: Villains: you did not so, when your vile daggers
   Hack'd one another in the sides of Caesar:
   You show'd your teeth like apes,
   And fawn'd like hounds,
   And bow'd like bondmen, kissing Caesar's feet;

Whilst damned Casca, like a cur, behind
Struck Caesar on the neck. O you flatterers.

CASSIUS: Flatterers? Now Brutus thank yourself,
This tongue had not offended so today,
If Cassius might have rul'd.

OCTAVIUS: Come, come, the cause. If arguing make us
sweat,
The proof of it will turn to redder drops:
Look, I draw a sword against conspirators,
When think you that the sword goes up again?
Never till Caesar's three and thirty wounds
Be well aveng'd; or till another Caesar
Have added slaughter to the sword of traitors.

BRUTUS: Caesar, thou canst not die by traitors' hands,
Unless thou bring'st them with thee.

OCTAVIUS: So I hope:
I was not born to die on Brutus' sword.

BRUTUS: O if thou wert the noblest of thy strain,
Young man, thou couldst not die more honourable.

CASSIUS: A peevish schoolboy, worthless of such honour
Join'd with a masker, and a reveller.

ANTONY: Old Cassius still.

OCTAVIUS: Come Antony: away:
Defiance traitors, hurl we in your teeth,
If you dare fight today, come to the field;
If not, when you have stomachs.
                    Exeunt Octavius, Antony and Army.

CASSIUS: Why now blow wind, swell billow,
And swim bark:
The storm is up, and all is on the hazard.

BRUTUS: Ho Lucilius, hark, a word with you.

LUCILIUS: My Lord.   *Lucilius and Messala stand forth.*

CASSIUS: Messala.

MESSALA: What says my General?

CASSIUS: Messala, this is my birth-day: as this very day
  Was Cassius born. Give me thy hand Messala:
  Be thou my witness, that against my will
  (As Pompey was) am I compell'd to set
  Upon one battle all our liberties.
  You know, that I held Epicurus strong,
  And his opinion: Now I change my mind,
  And partly credit things that do presage.
  Coming from Sardis, on our former ensign
  Two mighty eagles fell, and there they perch'd,
  Gorging and feeding from our soldiers' hands,
  Who to Philippi here consorted us:
  This morning are they fled away, and gone,
  And in their steads, do ravens, crows, and kites
  Fly o'er our heads, and downward look on us
  As we were sickly prey; their shadows seem
  A canopy most fatal, under which
  Our Army lies, ready to give up the ghost.

MESSALA: Believe not so.

CASSIUS: I but believe it partly,
  For I am fresh of spirit, and resolv'd
  To meet all perils, very constantly.

BRUTUS: Even so Lucilius.

CASSIUS: Now most noble Brutus,
  The gods today stand friendly, that we may
  Lovers in peace, lead on our days to age.
  But since the affairs of men rest still incertain,
  Let's reason with the worst that may befall.
  If we do lose this battle, then is this
  The very last time we shall speak together:
  What are you then determined to do?

BRUTUS: Even by the rule of that Philosophy,

By which I did blame Cato, for the death
Which he did give himself, I know not how:
But I do find it cowardly, and vile,
For fear of what might fall, so to prevent
The time of life, arming myself with patience,
To stay the providence of some high Powers,
That govern us below.

CASSIUS: Then, if we lose this battle,
You are contented to be led in triumph
Thorough the streets of Rome.

BRUTUS: No Cassius, no:
Think not thou noble Roman,
That ever Brutus will go bound to Rome,
He bears too great a mind. But this same day
Must end that work, the Ides of March begun.
And whether we shall meet again, I know not:
Therefore our everlasting farewell take:
For ever, and for ever, farewell Cassius,
If we do meet again, why we shall smile;
If not, why then this parting was well made.

CASSIUS: For ever, and for ever, farewell Brutus:
If we do meet again, we'll smile indeed;
If not, 'tis true, this parting was well made.

BRUTUS: Why then lead on. O that a man might know
The end of this day's business, ere it come:
But it sufficeth, that the day will end,
And then the end is known. Come ho, away.

Exeunt.

V.2

Alarum. Enter Brutus and Messala.

BRUTUS: Ride, ride Messala, ride and give these bills
  Unto the Legions, on the other side.

Loud alarum.

  Let them set on at once: for I perceive
  But cold demeanour in Octavius' wing:
  And sudden push gives them the overthrow:
  Ride, ride Messala, let them all come down.

Exeunt.

Alarums. Enter Cassius and Titinius.

CASSIUS: O look Titinius, look, the villains fly:
  Myself have to mine own turn'd enemy:
  This Ensign here of mine was turning back,
  I slew the coward, and did take it from him.

TITINIUS: O Cassius, Brutus gave the word too early,
  Who having some advantage on Octavius,
  Took it too eagerly: his soldiers fell to spoil,
  Whilst we by Antony are all enclos'd.

Enter Pindarus.

PINDARUS: Fly further off my Lord: fly further off,
  Mark Antony is in your tents my Lord:
  Fly therefore noble Cassius, fly far off.

CASSIUS: This hill is far enough. Look, look Titinius;
  Are those my tents where I perceive the fire?

TITINIUS: They are, my Lord.

CASSIUS: Titinius, if thou lovest me,
  Mount thou my horse, and hide thy spurs in him,
  Till he have brought thee up to yonder troops
  And here again, that I may rest assur'd
  Whether yond troops, are friend or enemy.

TITINIUS: I will be here again, even with a thought.
Exit.
CASSIUS: Go Pindarus, get higher on that hill,
  My sight was ever thick: regard Titinius,
  And tell me what thou not'st about the field.
Exit Pindarus.
  This day I breathed first, Time is come round,
  And where I did begin, there shall I end,
  My life is run his compass. Sirrah, what news?
PINDARUS [*Above*]: O my Lord.
CASSIUS: What news?
PINDARUS: Titinius is enclosed round about
  With horsemen, that make to him on the spur,
  Yet he spurs on. Now they are almost on him:
  Now Titinius. Now some light: O he lights too.
  He's ta'en.   *Shout.*
  And hark, they shout for joy.
CASSIUS: Come down, behold no more:
  O coward that I am, to live so long,
  To see my best friend ta'en before my face.
Enter Pindarus.
  Come hither sirrah: In Parthia did I take thee prisoner,
  And then I swore thee, saving of thy life,
  That whatsoever I did bid thee do,
  Thou shouldst attempt it. Come now, keep thine oath,
  Now be a free-man, and with this good sword
  That ran through Caesar's bowels, search this bosom.
  Stand not to answer: Here, take thou the hilts,
  And when my face is cover'd, as 'tis now,
  Guide thou the sword – Caesar, thou art reveng'd,
  Even with the sword that kill'd thee.   *Dies.*
PINDARUS: So, I am free,
  Yet would not so have been

Durst I have done my will. O Cassius,
Far from this country Pindarus shall run,
Where never Roman shall take note of him.   *Exit.*
                    Enter Titinius with Messala.

MESSALA: It is but change, Titinius: for Octavius
Is overthrown by noble Brutus' power,
As Cassius' Legions are by Antony.

TITINIUS: These tidings will well comfort Cassius.

MESSALA: Where did you leave him?

TITINIUS: All disconsolate,
With Pindarus his bondman, on this hill.

MESSALA: Is not that he that lies upon the ground?

TITINIUS: He lies not like the living. O my heart!

MESSALA: Is not that he?

TITINIUS: No, this was he Messala,
But Cassius is no more. O setting Sun:
As in thy red rays thou dost sink to night,
So in his red blood Cassius' day is set.
The Sun of Rome is set. Our day is gone,
Clouds, dews, and dangers come; our deeds are done:
Mistrust of my success hath done this deed.

MESSALA: Mistrust of good success hath done this deed.
O hateful Error, Melancholy's child:
Why dost thou show to the apt thoughts of men
The things that are not? O Error soon conceiv'd,
Thou never com'st unto a happy birth,
But kill'st the mother that engender'd thee.

TITINIUS: What Pindarus? Where art thou Pindarus?

MESSALA: Seek him Titinius, whilst I go to meet
The noble Brutus, thrusting this report
Into his ears; I may say thrusting it:
For piercing steel, and darts envenomed,
Shall be as welcome to the ears of Brutus,

As tidings of this sight.
TITINIUS: Hie you Messala,
And I will seek for Pindarus the while.
Exit Messala.
Why didst thou send me forth brave Cassius?
Did I not meet thy friends, and did not they
Put on my brows this wreath of victory,
And bid me give it thee? Didst thou not hear their shouts?
Alas, thou hast misconstrued every thing.
But hold thee, take this garland on thy brow,
Thy Brutus bid me give it thee, and I
Will do his bidding. Brutus, come apace,
And see how I regarded Caius Cassius:
By your leave Gods: This is a Roman's part,
Come Cassius' sword, and find Titinius' heart.   *Dies.*
   Alarum. Enter Brutus, Messala, young Cato, Strato,
       Volumnius, and Lucilius.
BRUTUS: Where, where Messala, doth his body lie?
MESSALA: Lo yonder, and Titinius mourning it.
BRUTUS: Titinius' face is upward.
CATO: He is slain.
BRUTUS: O Julius Caesar, thou art mighty yet,
Thy Spirit walks abroad, and turns our swords
In our own proper entrails.   *Low Alarums.*
CATO: Brave Titinius,
Look where he have not crown'd dead Cassius.
BRUTUS: Are yet two Romans living such as these?
The last of all the Romans, fare thee well:
It is impossible, that ever Rome
Should breed thy fellow. Friends I owe mo tears
To this dead man, than you shall see me pay.
I shall find time, Cassius: I shall find time.
Come therefore, and to Tharsus send his body,

His funerals shall not be in our camp,
Lest it discomfort us. Lucilius come,
And come young Cato, let us to the field,
Labeo and Flavius set our battles on:
'Tis three o'clock, and Romans yet ere night,
We shall try fortune in a second fight.

Exeunt.

V. 3

Alarum. Enter Brutus, Messala, Cato, Lucilius,
and Flavius.

BRUTUS: Yet Countrymen: O yet, hold up your heads.
CATO: What bastard doth not? Who will go with me?
   I will proclaim my name about the field.
   I am the son of Marcus Cato, ho.
   A foe to tyrants, and my Country's friend.
   I am the son of Marcus Cato, ho.

Enter soldiers, and fight.

BRUTUS: And I am Brutus, Marcus Brutus, I,
   Brutus my country's friend: Know me for Brutus.

Exit.

LUCILIUS: O young and noble Cato, art thou down?
   Why now thou diest, as bravely as Titinius,
   And may'st be honour'd, being Cato's son.
1 SOLDIER: Yield, or thou diest.
LUCILIUS: Only I yield to die:
   There is so much, that thou wilt kill me straight:
   Kill Brutus, and be honour'd in his death.
1 SOLDIER: We must not: a noble prisoner.

Enter Antony.

2 SOLDIER: Room ho: tell Antony, Brutus is ta'en.
1 SOLDIER: I'll tell the news. Here comes the General,

Brutus is ta'en, Brutus is ta'en my Lord.

ANTONY: Where is he?

LUCILIUS: Safe Antony, Brutus is safe enough:
    I dare assure thee, that no enemy
    Shall ever take alive the noble Brutus:
    The Gods defend him from so great a shame,
    When you do find him, or alive, or dead,
    He will be found like Brutus, like himself.

ANTONY: This is not Brutus friend, but I assure you,
    A prize no less in worth; keep this man safe,
    Give him all kindness. I had rather have
    Such men my friends, than enemies. Go on,
    And see where Brutus be alive or dead,
    And bring us word, unto Octavius' tent:
    How every thing is chanc'd.

Exeunt.

Enter Brutus, Dardanius, Clitus, Strato, and Volumnius.

BRUTUS: Come poor remains of friends, rest on this rock.

CLITUS: Statilius show'd the torch-light, but my Lord
    He came not back: he is or ta'en, or slain.

BRUTUS: Sit thee down, Clitus: slaying is the word,
    It is a deed in fashion. Hark thee, Clitus.

CLITUS: What I, my Lord? No, not for all the World.

BRUTUS: Peace then, no words.

CLITUS: I'll rather kill myself.

BRUTUS: Hark thee, Dardanius.

DARDANIUS: Shall I do such a deed?

CLITUS: O Dardanius.

DARDANIUS: O Clitus.

CLITUS: What ill request did Brutus make to thee?

DARDANIUS: To kill him, Clitus: look he meditates.

CLITUS: Now is that noble vessel full of grief,
    That it runs over even at his eyes.

BRUTUS: Come hither, good Volumnius, list a word.

VOLUMNIUS: What says my Lord?

BRUTUS: Why this, Volumnius:
The Ghost of Caesar hath appear'd to me
Two several times by night: at Sardis, once;
And this last night, here in Philippi fields:
I know my hour is come.

VOLUMNIUS: Not so, my Lord.

BRUTUS: Nay, I am sure it is, Volumnius.
Thou seest the world, Volumnius, how it goes,
Our enemies have beat us to the pit: *Low alarums.*
It is more worthy, to leap in ourselves,
Then tarry till they push us. Good Volumnius,
Thou know'st, that we two went to school together:
Even for that our love of old, I prithee
Hold thou my sword hilts, whilst I run on it.

VOLUMNIUS: That's not an office for a friend, my Lord.
                    Alarum still.

CLITUS: Fly, fly my Lord, there is no tarrying here.

BRUTUS: Farewell to you, and you, and you Volumnius.
Strato, thou hast been all this while asleep:
Farewell to thee too Strato, Countrymen:
My heart doth joy, that yet in all my life,
I found no man, but he was true to me.
I shall have glory by this losing day
More than Octavius, and Mark Antony,
By this vile conquest shall attain unto.
So fare you well at once, for Brutus' tongue
Hath almost ended his life's History:
Night hangs upon mine eyes, my bones would rest,
That have but labour'd, to attain this hour.
                    Alarum. Cry within, Fly, fly, fly.

CLITUS: Fly my Lord, fly.

BRUTUS: Hence: I will follow:
>   *Exeunt Clitus, Dardanius, and Volumnius.*
> I prithee Strato, stay thou by thy Lord,
> Thou art a fellow of a good respect:
> Thy life hath had some smatch of honour in it,
> Hold then my sword, and turn away thy face,
> While I do run upon it. Wilt thou Strato?

STRATO: Give me your hand first. Fare you well my Lord.

BRUTUS: Farewell good Strato. – Caesar, now be still,
> I kill'd not thee with half so good a will.   *Dies.*
>   *Alarum. Retreat. Enter Octavius, Antony, Messala,*
>   *Lucilius and the Army.*

OCTAVIUS: What man is that?

MESSALA: My Master's man: Strato, where is thy Master?

STRATO: Free from the bondage you are in Messala,
> The conquerors can but make a fire of him:
> For Brutus only overcame himself,
> And no man else hath honour by his death.

LUCILIUS: So Brutus should be found. I thank thee Brutus
> That thou hast prov'd Lucilius' saying true.

OCTAVIUS: All that serv'd Brutus, I will entertain them.
> Fellow, wilt thou bestow thy time with me?

STRATO: Ay, if Messala will prefer me to you.

OCTAVIUS: Do so, good Messala.

MESSALA: How died my Master, Strato?

STRATO: I held the sword, and he did run on it.

MESSALA: Octavius, then take him to follow thee,
> That did the latest service to my Master.

ANTONY: This was the noblest Roman of them all:
> All the Conspirators save only he,
> Did that they did, in envy of great Caesar:
> He, only in a general honest thought,
> And common good to all, made one of them.

His life was gentle, and the elements
So mix'd in him, that Nature might stand up,
And say to all the world; This was a man.
OCTAVIUS: According to his virtue, let us use him
With all respect, and rites of burial.
Within my tent his bones tonight shall lie,
Most like a soldier ordered honourably:
So call the field to rest, and let's away,
To part the glories of this happy day.

Exeunt omnes.

NOTES

References are to the page and line of this edition; there are 33 lines to the full page.

labouring day . . . profession: i.e., why are you out in the streets on a working day without your tools? P. 25 LL. 7–8

withal: with a pun on 'with awl'. P. 25 L. 29

climb'd up to walls: Throughout the play Shakespeare has rather his own London in mind than classical Rome. Such a sight as this was familiar. Thus, at the funeral of Queen Elizabeth, the 'city of Westminster was surcharged with multitudes of all sorts of people in their streets, houses, windows, leads "and gutters" that came to see the obsequy'. [John Stow's *Annals*.] P. 26 L. 15

for the course: i.e., stripped for running. Plutarch notes that at the feast of the Lupercalia many young men of good family ran naked through the streets, striking in sport those whom they passed. It was believed that women struck in this way would have a good delivery if pregnant, or if barren would conceive. P. 27 L. 23

Ides of March: March 15. P. 28 L. 15

of the best respect: most respected. P. 29 L. 29

stale . . . protester: 'to make my love worthless by swearing cheap oaths to everyone who claims to like me'. P. 30 LL. 10–11

hearts of controversy: eager rivalry. P. 31 L. 16

Aeneas . . . Anchises: According to the legend (which is the subject of Virgil's *Aeneid*) Aeneas was one of the few survivors of the capture of Troy. He carried off his old father Anchises, and sailed away with his company to Italy where he became the founder of the Roman race. P. 31 LL. 19–21

Colossus: the Colossus of Rhodes, one of the Seven Wonders of the Ancient World, was a great bronze statue straddling the entrance to the harbour. P. 32 L. 11

P. 32 L. 31   *Rome ... room:* both words were pronounced, and often spelt, alike.

P. 33. L. 1   *Brutus once:* i.e., Lucius Junius Brutus, who was chiefly responsible for the expulsion of Tarquin, the last king of Rome; after which Rome became a republic.

P. 33 L. 27   *look you Cassius:* Shakespeare was very sparing in his use of stage directions describing how his plays were to be produced; but here, as often, the action is indicated in the dialogue itself.

P. 36 L. 11   *doublet:* jacket. See note on P. 46 LL. 23–4.

P. 36 L. 12   *occupation:* trade, and so provided with a handy tool.

P. 37 L. 12   *tardy form:* appearance of slow wittedness.

P. 39 L. 31   *unbraced:* with the doublet loose. The doublet supported the hose with tagged laces which were normally drawn tight, or 'braced'. When taking his ease, or too hot, a man might loosen the doublet, as today he unbuttons his waistcoat.

P. 40 L. 16   *from quality and kind:* contrary to their nature and species.

P. 40 L. 23   *monstrous state:* unnatural state of affairs.

P. 40 L. 27   *lion in the Capitol:* See note on P. 48 L. 3.

P. 42 L. 7   *Be factious:* seditious, i.e., form a party.

P. 43 L. 7   *old Brutus:* See P. 33 L. 1.

P. 43 L. 21   *alchemy:* the principal aim of alchemy was to discover how to transmute base metals into gold.

P. 44 L. 2   *Enter Brutus in his orchard:* This is one of the very few Place Directions in the Folio. Those usually printed in modern editions of Shakespeare were added by editors.

P. 45 L. 2   *Will bear no colour:* cannot be justified.

P. 45 L. 24   *Shall Rome, &c.:* As the actor was provided with a written copy of the letter, there was no need to include it in his part.

P. 46 L. 13   *Genius, and the mortal instruments:* Here *genius* means the rational mind; the *mortal instruments* are the parts of the body which carry out the mind's decisions –

mortal because they decay in death, whilst the immortal soul survives.

little kingdom: the body of man – the microcosm or P. 46 L. 15
little universe – is often paralleled with the macrocosm, the great Universe. The same notion is elaborately worked out in Menenius' fable of the Belly and the Members in *Coriolanus* (I. 1).

hats . . . cloaks: The costuming of *Julius Caesar* is P. 46 LL.
Elizabethan. Shakespeare's Romans go about 'un- 23–4
braced', wear doublets, night-gowns, wide-brimmed
hats and cloaks.

thy native semblance on: in your natural grimness. P. 47 L. 2

Capitol: Shakespeare in his own mind identified the P. 48 L. 3
Capitol with the Tower of London, which also lay
conspicuously at the East end of the City. There were
kept the lions, which were one of the sights of London.

face of men: the downcast faces of men cowed by P. 48 L. 6
tyranny.

unicorns . . . trees: This failing in unicorns is thus P. 51 L. 3
described by Spenser:
'Like as a Lion, whose imperial power
  A proud rebellious Unicorn defies,
  T'avoid the rash assault and wrathful stour
  Of his fierce foe, him to a tree applies,
  And when him running in full course he spies,
  He slips aside; the whiles that furious beast
  His precious horn, sought of his enemies,
  Strikes in the stock, ne thence can be releas'd
But to the mighty victor yields a bounteous feast.'
              [*Faery Queen*, II, v, 10.]

honey-heavy dew: a mixed metaphor. 'Honey-dew' P. 51 L. 32
is the spot of sweet moisture exuded by some flowers. 'Sleep' is 'dewy' because it falls lightly; but
'honey-heavy' because it is also sweet and overwhelming.

sick offence: a trouble causing sickness. P. 53 L. 7

Am I yourself . . . sometimes: 'Am I your mate only P. 53 LL.
on terms and conditions which allow me merely to 22–5

eat, sleep and talk with you, but not to share your secrets and anxieties?'

P. 53 L. 26   *in the suburbs*: the outskirts. The suburbs of London were haunts of harlots.

P. 54 L. 16   *charactery*: symbols; one form of Elizabethan short-hand was called 'Charactery'. *Charactery . . . brows*: that which is symbolized by my sad looks.

P. 54 L. 26   *wear a kerchief*: i.e., to muffle yourself as an invalid.

P. 55 L. 19   *in his night-gown*: i.e., dressing-gown.

P. 56 L. 4   *Caesar shall forth*: Like other stage tyrants, Julius Caesar speaks of himself pompously in the third person.

P. 57 L. 10   *We are two*: The Folio reads 'We heare two'.

P. 58 L. 10   *statue*: pronounced as three syllables.

P. 58 LL. 22–3   *great men . . . cognizance*: Decius interprets the dream in a double sense. To Caesar he implies that men shall seek honours (in the form of heraldic coats-of-arms or *tinctures*), mementoes, and badges (*cognizance*) denoting that they are his servants. His true meaning is that they shall preserve relics of his death, for it was a pious custom to dip handkerchiefs in the blood of those who were executed for their religious or political principles. (See P. 77 LL. 14–19.)

P. 58 L. 31   *Apt to be render'd*: likely to be made.

P. 59 L. 5   *reason to . . . liable*: my discretion gives way to my love (and makes me say things which may offend).

P. 62 L. 18   III. 1. The Act division, though it is marked in the Folio, is unfortunate, for there is no real pause in the action until after III. 1.

P. 63 L. 3   *Sirrah*: a term of address used to an inferior.

P. 64 LL. 3–4   *pre-ordinance . . . children*: 'law' is the usual emendation for the Folio reading 'lane'. Caesar means 'ordinary men might be moved by your pleading, but my will has the force of that which is ordained from the first and does not change capriciously like the will of a child'.

P. 64 L. 8   *spaniel fawning*: Shakespeare elsewhere uses the spaniel as an image of servile flattery.

Ambition's debt is paid: Caesar has paid for his ambi-   P. 65 L. 20
tion.

Pompey's basis: the base of Pompey's statue.   P. 66 L. 23

untrod state: new state of affairs, as yet without a path. P. 67 L. 14

let blood ... rank: periodical blood-letting was con-   P. 68 L. 1
sidered good for the general health. *rank:* in a condition requiring blood-letting.

Our arms in strength of malice: a difficult phrase. If the P. 68 L. 23
Folio reading is correct then it means 'having the
power to do harm'.

disposing ... dignities: The contrast between Brutus P. 68 L. 27
and Cassius is here well shown. Brutus offers Antony
fine sentiments, Cassius a share in the spoils.

Sign'd ... lethe: both phrases are hunting terms and P. 69 L. 23
mean the same – 'marked with thy death blood'.

prick'd: marked in the list. The names of those select- P. 70 L. 1
ed were at one time actually pricked with a pin: the
phrase is still used in the 'pricking (or selection) of
sheriffs'.

Ate: goddess of mischief.   P. 71 L. 29

Cry havoc: 'no mercy' – i.e., no prisoners will be P. 71 L. 31
taken.

general coffers: public treasury.   P. 75 L. 33

a worse come in his place: Shakespeare's variant of the P. 76 LL.
old proverb 'seldom cometh better'.   22–3

dip their napkins: See note on P. 58 LL. 22–3.   P. 77 L. 15

overcame the Nervii: one of the hardest fought of all P. 78 L. 22
Caesar's battles in Gaul.

Caesar's angel: one whom Caesar regarded as his P. 78 L. 30
guardian angel.

marr'd ... with traitors: destroyed by traitors.   P. 79 L. 13

writ: a speech written out and carefully prepared. P. 80 L. 5
Many editors emend to 'wit'.

unluckily ... fantasy: burden my imagination with P. 82 L. 4
foreboding of bad luck.

bear me a bang: get a blow from me.   P. 82 L. 19

corporal motion: bodily action.   P. 84 L. 20

P. 84 L. 24   *abjects, orts :* the generally accepted emendation for 'objects, arts'. *abjects :* worthless things; *orts :* scraps of food.

P. 84 L. 31   *means stretch'd :* our resources used to the full.

P. 85 L. 2   *at the stake :* i.e., like the bear baited by the hounds. Bear-baiting was a popular sport, and the Bear Garden was quite near to the Globe Theatre.

P. 85 L. 16   *In his own change :* because he has degenerated. Sometimes emended to *charge :* by his own order.

P. 85 L. 26   *familiar instances :* friendly actions.

P. 86 L. 1   *enforced ceremony :* forced politeness.

P. 86 LL. 3–8   *horses . . . trial :* like horses which are restless when the rider wishes them to stand but tire quickly when spurred on; *fall their crests :* become crestfallen.

P. 87 L. 10   *slighted off :* dismissed as slight matters.

P. 88 L. 4   *hedge me in :* restrain me.

P. 88 L. 22   *observe you :* i.e., be careful of your moods.

P. 90 L. 17   *conn'd by rote :* learned by heart.

P. 90 L. 21   *Pluto :* for Plutus, the god of riches.

P. 91 L. 28   *I'll . . . time :* I'll regard his whims when he obtrudes them at the proper time.

P. 93 L. 31   *dead . . . manner :* There seems to be a discrepancy in the text here, for Brutus has already told Cassius of the manner of Portia's death. The likeliest explanation is that this scene has been revised, and, as often happened in the printing of Shakespeare's texts, both corrected and revised passages were printed. If the text is correct, then Shakespeare presumably intended to exhibit Brutus deliberately showing off his stoicism.

P. 94 L. 3   *in Art as you :* The contrast between 'Art' (that which is acquired by training) and 'Nature' (that which is inborn) is common. Cassius means that he could deliberately force himself to be patient in such a trial, but it would not be natural.

P. 96 L. 12   *pocket of my gown :* another instance of Elizabethan costume.

Lay'st . . . leaden mace: the metaphor is from the offi- P. 96 L. 29
cer who touches the prisoner with his mace of office
as a token of arrest. *Leaden* is a common image for
sleep, denoting 'dull' and 'heavy'.

battles: armies drawn up ready for battle. P. 98 L. 16

in their bosoms: can interpret their thoughts. P. 98 L. 19

fearful bravery: brave merely in show. P. 98 L. 22

Hybla: a mountain in Sicily famous for its honey. P. 99 L. 23

masker: one who spends his time in midnight revel- P. 100 L. 20
ling and masquerades.

Epicurus: Epicurus warned his disciples not to believe P. 101 L. 7
in omens and other popular superstitions.

prevent . . . life: forestall the natural end of life by P. 102 LL.
suicide. 4–5

Ensign . . . it from him: Ensign was used both for the P. 103 LL.
company colours and the officer who carried them. 14–15

Pindarus [above]: i.e., on the upper Stage. P. 104 L. 10

Error, Melancholy's child: the word 'melancholy' was P. 105 L. 23
used not merely to denote sadness or depression, but
all forms of mental disturbance believed to arise from
excess of black bile. Acute melancholy produced hal-
lucination.

Tharsus: the Folio reading. The editors usually alter P. 106 L. 33
to Thasos.

second fight: Actually there were two battles at P. 106 L. 6
Philippi, the second twenty days after the first.

elements So mix'd in him: It was believed that the P. 111 LL.
human body and nature consisted of the four primary 1–2
elements or principles of earth, air, fire, and water.
Each of these elements affected a man's body and
mind in different ways. In perfect man all four were
exactly balanced.

GLOSSARY

address'd: prepared
ague: fever
apprehensive: intelligent

battles: forces
bay'd: brought to bay
bent: inclination
bills: written messages
bravery: show of bravery
bustling: indistinct

call in question: consider
cautelous: crafty
ceremonies: (1) symbols of honour; (2) superstitious beliefs
check'd: rebuked
choler: anger
chopt: chapped
closet: small room, study
common: public
companion: like 'fellow' used sometimes in a derogatory sense
conceit: think
conference: debate
consorted: accompanied
constancy: firmness
contrive: plot
cull out: choose to take

dint: stroke
disjoins: separates

earns: yearns, grieves
element: sky

enforc'd: stressed
enfranchisement: liberty
engag'd: pledged
envy: hatred
Erebus: Hell
even: steady
exhalations: meteors
exigent: crisis
extenuated: diminished

faction: members of the party
faculties: natural qualities
fain: gladly
falling sickness: epilepsy
favour: face
fearful: timid
fleering: timid
fond: foolish
formal: dignified
former: foremost
fret: cover with stripes

general: general good
glaz'd: glared

happy: lucky
high-sighted: arrogant
hinds: deer
humour: (1) whim; (2) dampness

indifferently: impartially
indirection: underhand means
insuppressive: not to be suppressed
issue: action

jades: feeble-spirited horses
jealous: suspicious

laughter: cause of jesting, jester
leaden: blunt
lief: soon
lottery: turn

mark of favour: characteristic of face
mart: market
mean: means
mechanical: working man
misconstrued: misinterpreted
mo: more
mock: jibe
mortified: dead

neat: ox
niggard: grudgingly allow
noted: publicly censured

occupation: handicraft
o'er-watched: tired out
ope: open

passion: emotion
path: walk
physical: healthy
pitch: flight
present: immediate
prevention: discovery
prick'd: marked down in the list

proper: individual, own

remorse: pity
replication: echo
resolv'd: informed
rheumy: damp
riv'd: split

security: lack of precaution
sensible: sensitive
several: separate
shadow: reflection
smatch: taste
soil: blemish
stare: stand on end
stomachs: appetites

taper: candle
thorough: through
thunder-stone: thunderbolt
toils: traps
trash: twigs, kindling
tributaries: vanquished prisoners who have agreed to pay tribute

unmeritable: without merit
unnumber'd: innumerable
urged: brought forward
use: custom

void: empty

where: whether.

PENGUIN POPULAR CLASSICS

Published or forthcoming

PENGUIN POPULAR CLASSICS

Published or forthcoming

PENGUIN POPULAR CLASSICS

Published or forthcoming

Herman Melville	Moby Dick
Francis Turner Palgrave	The Golden Treasury
Edgar Allan Poe	Selected Tales
Walter Scott	Ivanhoe
William Shakespeare	Antony and Cleopatra
	As You Like It
	Hamlet
	King Lear
	Macbeth
	The Merchant of Venice
	A Midsummer Night's Dream
	Othello
	Romeo and Juliet
	The Tempest
	Twelfth Night
Mary Shelley	Frankenstein
Robert Louis Stevenson	Dr Jekyll and Mr Hyde
	Kidnapped
	Treasure Island
Bram Stoker	Dracula
Jonathan Swift	Gulliver's Travels
W. M. Thackeray	Vanity Fair
Anthony Trollope	Barchester Towers
	Framley Parsonage
	The Warden
Mark Twain	Huckleberry Finn
	Tom Sawyer
Jules Verne	Around the World in Eighty Days
	Twenty Thousand Leagues Under the S
Oscar Wilde	Lord Arthur Saville's Crime
	The Picture of Dorian Gray